Cinders

METTE BACH

JAMES LORIMER & COMPANY LTD., PUBLISHERS
TORONTO

James Lorimer & Company Ltd., Publishers acknowledges funding support from the Ontario Arts Council (OAC), an agency of the Government of Ontario. We acknowledge the support of the Canada Council for the Arts, which last year invested $153 million to bring the arts to Canadians throughout the country. This project has been made possible in part by the Government of Canada and with the support of the Ontario Media Development Corporation.

Cover design: Tyler Cleroux
Cover image: Shutterstock

Library and Archives Canada Cataloguing in Publication

Bach, Mette, 1976-, author
        Cinders / Mette Bach.

(Real love)
Issued in print and electronic formats.
ISBN 978-1-4594-1383-2 (softcover).--ISBN 978-1-4594-1384-9 (EPUB)

        I. Title. II. Series: Real love (Series)

PS8603.A298C55 2018   jC813'.6   C2018-902565-4
                                                   C2018-902566-2

Published by: Distributed in Canada by: Distributed in the US by:
James Lorimer &   Formac Lorimer Books   Lerner Publisher Services
Company Ltd., Publishers   5502 Atlantic Street   1251 Washington Ave. N.
117 Peter Street, Suite 304   Halifax, NS, Canada   Minneapolis, MN, USA
Toronto, ON, Canada   B3H 1G4   55401
M5V 0M3   www.lernerbooks.com
www.lorimer.ca

Printed and bound in Canada.
Manufactured by Friesens Corporation in Altona, Manitoba,
Canada in July 2018.
Job # 245777

For Billeh Nickerson for being the closest thing to a Fairy Godmother I've ever had.

PROLOGUE

Phoenix

ASH REMEMBERED THE WORDS of her mother. "The phoenix is living flame. Once it burns down to embers, it will rise again and be reborn. Whenever your life seems to turn to ashes, it's really a new start. That's why I named you Ashley. That's where your name comes from."

Ash's birth was what some people would have called an accident. Ash's mom liked to call it the greatest miracle of her life. When her mom met Ted, who would become Ash's stepfather, she told him that her daughter was more important than any man in her life. She used to tell Ash that no romantic love could hold a candle to the love between a mother and child.

Ash and her mom talked about everything from myths to hairstyles, from making art to making muffins. They watched Oprah together and danced to music videos together. They were so close, they seemed to share one life instead of two. So now that her mom was gone, Ash was torn up inside. A part of her had died right alongside her mom. Her mom might have been the one who was cremated, but Ash, the part of her still living and breathing, felt like the pile of ashes. The ashes from which she had to rise again.

01 Once Upon a Time

ASH'S ARMS WERE HEAVY with garbage. She carried the huge bag out to the bin behind the big house. How had the family managed to create so much waste in just one week? She knew it was mostly the take-out containers and leftovers from her mother's funeral. Somehow, that made it even heavier.

Ash's stepsister, Mimi, aimed her phone at Ash. *Not this again*, thought Ash. It had been going on for months, Mimi snapping photos of Ash holding garbage, taking out garbage. At first, it was at school where Ash worked in the cafeteria. It started as a way for Mimi to crack up her friends. But soon Mimi found that posting the pictures online could make her Mean Queen of social media. She added pics of Ash doing chores around the house where Ash and her mother lived with Mimi's father, Ted, and brother, Noah. Mimi documented all Ash's garbage disposal and dubbed her Garbage Girl. All of it for the Instagram account Mimi used to ridicule people at their school. It was the exact reverse of Humans of New York. They called it Dorks of North Delta. Ash had no time for it. She sighed and glared at Mimi.

"Really, Mimi? The garbage from my mom's funeral?" she said. She tossed the heavy black bag into the bin. "Really?"

Mimi just laughed.

"You're not hurting me, you know," Ash said. "But I worry about you. This isn't exactly your best self."

Even in the depth of her own sorrow, Ash tried to feel sorry for Mimi. It wasn't that she loved Mimi — she absolutely didn't. But she was haunted by something her mom had said. Her mom told Ash to be kind to people who didn't know how to be kind themselves.

Mimi rolled her eyes. "Whatever."

"Whatever indeed."

Ash was the same age as Mimi and her twin brother, Noah. But Ash had always been too busy to be as immature as her stepsiblings. It was easier for Ash to accept they lived on a different planet from hers and to just stay out of their way.

After her chores were done, Ash sat by the fireplace. She could see herself in the highly polished metal. She looked sad and tired. While she read a book on computer programming languages, Mimi came and snapped another shot of her. Ash would see it later that day, posted to Mimi's Instagram account with the caption, *Poor little orphan girl.*

Mimi and Noah each had a huge bedroom with a bathroom. Ash stayed in the guest bedroom, which was still used mostly for storage. A year after she and her mom had moved in, the room was still full of boxes. Ted had told her to make herself at home. But it didn't feel like home. Home was where she and her mom lived until her mom's cancer got so bad that they couldn't live on their own. Ted proposed to Ash's mom as a final romantic gesture after years of the on-again-off-again thing they had. So now Ash was left here with these kids who were supposed to be her family. Kids who didn't like Ash.

The morning that Ash was heading back to school after her mom's death, she found Noah in the kitchen. He was eating a prepared meal from Choices Market. Ash wasn't a guest in the house anymore. But she didn't feel right opening cupboards to look for cereal. Noah ignored her just standing there as he sat on the tall stool by the counter and downed his meal.

No way was Ash opening the fridge. After listening to Noah chew for what seemed like an hour, she noticed an apple in the fruit basket on the counter. It looked like it was for decoration. She didn't care. She had to eat something. So she took it.

Ted came downstairs. He nodded his head in Ash's direction and said to Noah, "You're driving her to school."

Ash wished he hadn't done that. It was her first day back after a week of grief leave. She wanted to ease back to her old life in her own way by taking the bus. But now Noah had to look at her. Ash and Noah lived their lives across a divide. Aside from their parents being connected, they had nothing in common.

Noah grunted in protest. It was clear he didn't want her riding with him any more than she did. "I have to pick up Sam, too. And I'm already giving Mimi a ride."

"So?" Ted said. "You have four seats in your car."

"Like a taxi," Noah huffed. He hopped off the chair and left the kitchen. Just before he was out of view, he looked back at Ash. "Be at the front door at quarter past eight."

Ash nodded.

This wasn't her life. It couldn't be. She would make it work because she had to. But she would not kid herself about them ever being a family. She knew Noah from the last two years of coding class. While Ash was busy trying to build an app, Noah was at the back of the room, shooting his mouth off about his car. The very car she'd now have to sit in.

Ash stood by the front door, with her shoes laced up. She thought about how her mom taught her to tie her shoes when she was little. When she thought of all the things her mom wasn't there to teach her now, she burst into tears. Her mom had been more like a sister to her. People had said they looked alike. They had slept in bunk beds in the old apartment. Ash wondered how she could deal with losing both her mother and her best friend.

Ted put his arm around Ash. She felt she barely knew him and she knew her mom didn't love him, not for real. But she let him hold her. She buried her face in Ted's chest and sobbed into his shirt.

"Where's she going to go now?" Noah asked.

"Now that her mom . . ."

"Nowhere," Ted said.

"She's staying here?"

"She's Mary's daughter. We can't very well let her be homeless, can we?"

Noah shrugged. "Don't see why not."

They talked like she wasn't even there, which made Ash cry all the more. She wished that she wasn't there. She wished she wasn't alive at all. Everything was awful.

"There's only a few months of school left," Ash managed to say. "I'll be out of here by June."

02 Earning Her Keep

THAT NIGHT, NOAH AND MIMI barged into Ash's room.

"Our dad's letting you stay here," Mimi said. "But don't expect a free ride."

"To school?" Ash asked.

"In life," Noah said. "We'll put up with you being around. But we have chores and they're not going to do themselves."

"You'll be pitching in," Mimi echoed.

Ash had already taken to tidying up, taking out

recycling, cleaning the bathrooms, and vacuuming. But she agreed to do some extra work. She would have without being asked.

"You start now," Noah said. "I'm going to need you to finish this assignment." He tossed his brand new MacBook Pro on her bed. "It's due tomorrow."

The twins turned and left.

Ash wanted to have another cry. But she thought that her mom would have wanted her to help out. That's what she always did. And besides, it was a simple coding assignment, the kind of thing Ash could do without trying. It was just distracting enough to keep her mind off of everything else. She was done by two in the morning.

The warning bell rang through the cafeteria. Ash had her hands in greasy water in the dish sink. She plucked dirty cups from the bin and sponged plates clean to run them through the sanitizer. She could already sense she'd be late for class. Her chest was tight because she found it hard to breathe when she was late.

"You're not going until they're all done," her boss said.

"Of course not," Ash replied. Very quietly, she added, "It's just that I have fifteen minutes. And I need to change and get to the other side of school and . . ."

Sally, a woman with severe frown lines, picked up a bowl from the tray air-drying on the back counter.

"This will have to go through once more."

"But . . ." Ash said. She knew better than to finish the sentence. She looked closely at the bowl, but could find nothing wrong with it. Sally was just in a mood. That happened a lot.

"Okay," Ash said. She gave up all hope that she'd get to class on time. She needed the pay she got for the job. It was one thing that Ted was letting her stay with them. But she would need money if she was going to attend the best coding school in the province.

By the time Ash got to class, Mr. Basra was explaining the final project. "This is your year-end, so remember that it has to be good. The best project will receive the prestigious Keener Scholarship, which includes first-year tuition and a cash award at graduation."

Ash slinked into her seat and tried to go unnoticed. It was awful being late. Noah was sitting with his entourage all around him. They took up a lot of space. They all sat with their arms behind their heads like they were lounging around a pool. Ash figured Noah probably did spend more time at the pool than anywhere else.

The whole gang of them in their pastel polo shirts never had to work, not like Ash did. Not doing gross stuff like dishes. Ash knew how Noah lived, how his dad got him everything down to laundry service and chopped fruit. She saw he wasn't expecting to ever have to do anything himself. That was why it made sense when he looked at her as if she was a waitress whose only purpose was to bring him a pop. And she knew he would go for the scholarship just because it would look good.

Ash had to get that scholarship. Her whole future depended on it.

That night Ash was fixing more kinks on the app she was working on. She was exhausted from having gone to her job, then to her classes, then to the library for homework, then home to do the vacuuming and take out the recycling. Sure enough, Noah came in without knocking.

"So I have this idea for the year-end. I need you to execute it. You heard Basra. It has to be good."

Ash was unsure how to tell Noah just how wrong it was for him to drop this on her. He was planning to cheat his way through the most important part of their last year of high school. Not to mention that she had her own project.

"I don't think I can help you," Ash said. She was surprised by the firmness in her voice.

"You don't have a choice."

She was equally surprised by the threat in his.

"Everyone has choices," Ash said.

"The way I see it, you're one step away from

being homeless. If that happens, how do you have a shot at a scholarship? No more coding dreams. You lose everything."

It was the truth. She needed to apply herself one hundred per cent if she wanted to compete with the likes of Noah to get into a decent school and get tuition paid for. It had always been the plan. Her mom's plan. Her plan. Their plan. Unlike Noah, Ash had grown up without money. The only thing her mom left her was the knowledge that she had to make it on her own.

"And you know my dad believes everything I tell him," Noah went on. "So that one step is me. You're one bad move away from me getting you kicked out. So I'd think twice about saying no."

Ash looked down. He might as well have a gun.

"Fine," she said. "What's your idea?"

"I'm still working on it, but it's brilliant. I'll tell you soon." He closed the door on his way out.

03 *Need Love*

"MIMI, WHAT ARE YOU ON ABOUT?" Noah asked over the meal Ted had brought home.

"Look at this," Mimi said. She shoved her phone in Noah's face. "That cow Char Gill does not deserve to have her video go viral. How's anyone supposed to compete with that?"

"That's a lot of likes," he confirmed.

"And for what? Singing someone else's song?" Mimi said.

Ted looked at his kids and put his hands up, saying, "I don't even want to know."

"Some chick that Mimi worships had a video go viral," Noah explained.

Ted looked confused. "I'm glad this social media stuff wasn't around when I was your age."

Ash looked at her plate. She moved a forkful of Thai food around it. She thought about how different things would be if she didn't have technology. No coding. No programming. Talk about the dark ages.

The cord of Ash's old laptop was tangled. When she unravelled the knot, she saw that the wire was exposed. She made a mental note to buy some electrical tape. Maybe duct tape. No way could she afford a new computer. She couldn't think about that now. She had to focus. She had asked Mr. Basra about some problems she was having with SendLove that day in school. It was the app she was doing for extra credit. Although they had tried to diagram it out on the whiteboard, Ash knew she just had to work through it.

Once again, Ash came up against a snag. So she let herself get distracted by her newsfeeds. Katrina Thompson, one of Ash's favourite YouTubers and a self-taught coder, had uploaded a new video. This one was about how coding boot camps were a waste of money and not necessary. Ash couldn't afford to go to one and Noah had gone for the past four summers in a row. So this was proof that what Ash wanted to do could be done. She listened while Katrina Thompson explained that you could learn coding online and get work in the field if you were disciplined. Girls like Katrina were everything to Ash. They made her future seem possible.

Then Ash made the mistake of looking at the comments. It sent a pang of despair through her to see mean comments beneath the video. Some random jerks somewhere attacked Katrina, not for her words, but for daring to be a woman. For daring to be a black woman, talking about tech. The words, like swords, were meant to stab. They were meant to hurt. It was clear that whoever wrote them had no interest in what Katrina had to say. All they cared about was being hateful. To Ash, that was not okay. She looked at the comments below Katrina's post and pictured the kind of slime who'd say stuff like that. It was cowardly to sit on the sidelines and criticize. Where was that person's video? How was that guy putting himself out there? The answer was that he wasn't. The world was divided into the people who did stuff and the people who made fun of them.

It was the very problem that Ash was trying to address with SendLove. And it was the push she needed to get offline and continue working on it.

Somehow seven hours passed. Ash was in the zone. There was something about coding that calmed her mind. The work almost did itself, and she reached a tranquil state where she wasn't stressed. It was like she could just watch things unfold before her.

It was four in the morning when SendLove was done. Ash had spent months and months toiling away on it. She and her mom had clung to the vision of

Ash making it one day in tech. Ash had kept at it in the face of all her sadness and loss. She'd poured the deep feelings that threatened to send her into a pit of despair into getting things just right. And now she sat there, unable to do anything but feel how huge it was. On SendLove, you could call on your community to drown out negativity with good stuff. You could battle haters with hope and love and support.

Ash posted a comment on Katrina's post with a link to SendLove. And she explained how it worked. When people left mean comments, SendLove members could stand up to the jerks together so no one had to feel alone and unsafe. Now all that was left was for Ash to join her own community. She'd been busy designing everything from the backend and going by Admin. She scratched her chin and tried to come up with something to represent herself.

Instead of a photo of her face, Ash uploaded a picture of her glasses. And she would need a name — not her real name. She thought about what her mom had told her about the phoenix dying and being reborn in flame. She thought about being named after what actually was transformed in the process. Ash. Embers. No, Cinders. Yes, that was it. She would be Cinders.

The next day, Ash yawned her way through her shift at the cafeteria. She barely kept awake for her classes. It wasn't until her spare block just after two that she even checked the app. Forty-three people were registered. The first name Ash saw on the list was Katrina Thompson. Her own hero and mentor had signed up for an account. There she was, front and centre. She'd signed up with her adorable avatar with pink hair that she used all over the Internet. In Ash's private inbox was a message from Katrina.

Great concept! Congrats on the launch. I told some friends at work. Hope you don't mind. And thanks for the love in the comments section. That guy's been trolling me on different sites for a long time.

Wow. Incredible. A message from Katrina was the best thumbs-up Ash could think of. It was a kind gesture to get a bunch of the right people on board with the app right away. Ash felt it was something her mother would have done. There was a cosiness about the way SendLove was spreading. It was like the whole thing was still a secret. But it wasn't. It was real now.

04 Send Love

IT WAS ALMOST IMPOSSIBLE for Ash to pay attention to her classes the next day. Her mind was racing with what the app meant. It was like she'd been let into a club. At school, she never felt let in. When people talked to her, it was usually just at her job. They wanted gravy with their fries or extra teriyaki sauce on their lunch. It wasn't ever about her or how she was doing.

In the library, Ash held her phone in her hand with the app open. She was daydreaming about a future where she worked with Katrina. They would talk about ideas, then put on some music and get down to it. They would sit side by side, nerding out for hours, only taking breaks to get re-inspired over coffee.

Suddenly there was a loud *thwap*. A heavy textbook came crashing down on the table in front of Ash. She was jolted back to reality and found Noah standing behind her.

"What are you doing?" he asked. "I've got some chemistry homework and it's due next period. I totally forgot."

"Well," Ash said, "I'm busy."

"You don't look busy," he said. He snatched Ash's phone from her as if it was his right to look at her text messages. "What's this?"

"Nothing."

He tossed the phone on the table. "I need that lab done in the next hour."

"Noah, you can't just expect me to drop everything to do your homework. What if I wasn't in here?"

"It's the library. Where else would you be?"

"I could be working. Or, I dunno. Out."

He didn't look amused. "I'll be back before the end of the period," he said as he left.

Ash sat there feeling stunned. Used. Noah was being a jerk, and she was letting him. She didn't know what else to do.

Ash did the assignment. It was easier to do it than to stand up to Noah. She didn't want it to get to the point where he would bring up the fact that she had nobody and nothing. It was true. And it was very hard for Ash to accept. The periodic table of elements was a lot easier to deal with than Noah.

Every now and then, Ash spaced out and checked her phone again. Slightly scared of the sudden success of SendLove, she couldn't go on just yet. She was sure there were still glitches. And someone would have to moderate the discussion board. But she was nervous after the fact. It was like the birthday party her mom threw for her when she turned twelve. Ash hadn't thought anyone would come at all, but a ton of people had. It made it hard for Ash to enjoy the party. She had already decided she shouldn't.

She browsed social media. Everyone looked busy enjoying life. Except her. She scrolled through the cute photos of girls who had made their eyes big and added pink cat ears. She looked at pictures of people at parties. Even pictures taken in the hallway outside the library at this school made it seem like there was a party going on. The party was always where she was not. That was the one part of social media she could rely on. She was never in the midst of anything.

Ash thought about Mimi's ambitions to become a social media queen. Even though Ash sometimes wondered what it would be like to care about that, she was glad she didn't. It seemed like the whole thing was a sham. They were an illusion of togetherness. The glossy photos made most people feel separate from the pack and caused them to try desperately to belong.

Noah came back, this time with two of his friends in tow.

"You done?" he asked.

He didn't wait for an answer. He snatched the papers from the desk in front of Ash and walked away. His friends laughed. Noah must have told them about her doing his work. That meant they knew she was a pushover. They knew she had nothing and nobody. That was very dangerous with guys like that. Ash wasn't scared that they would harm her, but she saw them for what they were: predators.

It wasn't until Ash was on the bus heading back to Ted's house that she was able to look at SendLove again. She put in her ear buds, even though she wasn't listening to anything. She wanted to be in her own world and ear buds sent that signal.

The numbers were up. Eighty-nine people were now listed as active users. It seemed unreal.

The app hosted a discussion board so members could write about their experiences of being targeted online. Katrina led the first thread. She talked about the troll whose comments had prompted Ash to put SendLove out there. She said that you can't let trolls hold you back. They're just like the nagging voices in your own head telling you you're not good enough. Not smart enough. Not pretty enough. Those voices would control you unless you learned how to drown them out. And so would trolls.

Ash got teary right there on the bus. She looked out the window at North Delta, the suburb that no longer felt like home. She might never feel at home again without her mom. She had learned to live without her dad, but she doubted very much that life without her mom could ever feel like real life. But as she read her hero's words, she realized that there was kindness. Not right in her own life, but not too far away. There were good people. And she had found a way to bring them to her.

When she got home, Ash signed in as Cinders to moderate the discussion board. She didn't want to police the talk. But she wanted to keep things moving. It was one thing she'd learned from years of being on and running discussion boards. If you saw people starting to write essays and you responded with essays, it would turn into everyone writing essays. The point of SendLove was to get positive energy to people who were being drowned in negative comments. Ash wanted to drive traffic where it needed to be.

And who was this? Someone named Charming had sent a message to her inbox.

Charming: Must be nice to be so cheerful.

Ash was stunned. Did she seem cheerful? There she was, feeling like she could barely breathe the air of a world that didn't include her mother. And someone thought she was cheerful. Ash could take the comment as snarky. But this was SendLove. And there was something wistful about the message. Ash decided to take it as praise. Maybe someone needed her to be cheerful. She could do that. She sent a message back that she was just keeping things positive, and added a funny emoji.

Back on the discussion board, Katrina asked Ash, under the Admin handle, what made her want to launch SendLove. Ash didn't normally open up about stuff online. Well, anywhere. But it seemed like a fair question and she wanted to answer. Without naming Mimi, she told the group that she was often targeted by a mean girl on social media.

And there was Charming on the discussion board.

Charming: I post a lot — selfies, videos. I mean, everyone does. For me it's part of getting where I want to take my life. I've never bullied anyone. I don't think I've even made a negative comment. But honesty is important here. I sometimes think that social media attention is too important to me.

How brave of Charming to put that out there, thought Ash. Charming needed her to make SendLove a safe place for that kind of risk. Ash was surprised to find that it cheered her up. So she steered the discussion in that direction.

05 *Survival*

THE NEXT DAY, after dinner and cleaning, Ash was thinking about her year-end project. She sat cross-legged on the bed, hunched over her old laptop. Her computer was so old that it could barely run the software she needed. Somehow she had to design something simple enough to work, but exciting enough to get her out into the world. Her eyes glazed over. She'd had so much screen time that day that she could barely stand to look at the computer much longer. But she felt there was a breakthrough coming.

Oh, here's a welcome distraction, Ash thought. Someone wanted to chat on SendLove. It was Charming.

Charming: Ugh.

Cinders: ???

Charming: My life. I'm kind of feeling like I'm not in the driver's seat.

Cinders: What happened?

Charming: I'm trying to figure out what I want to be. But I know I don't want to be what some people think I should be.

Cinders: Relatable.

Charming: And what if I change my mind? Everyone thinks that what's out there is the real me. And maybe it's not.

Cinders: I thought I was the only one. But maybe we're not talking about the same thing.

Charming: Sorry to be cryptic. Takes me a while to open up to anyone.

Cinders: Me too.

Ash was surprised that she really did want to open up. Who was this person with a life that seemed to be like hers? Ash was glad that she had listened to the part of her that wanted to be kind to Charming. Something made her want to reach out and tell this person that they were fine. Something made her want to follow up on this connection. But it was too much at this early stage. She didn't want to come across as needy or desperate. It was good enough — great, in fact — that Charming was there.

The reality was that Ash had no time for friendship or connection in real life. She had one focus. She needed to survive. She needed to get her schoolwork done. She needed to earn herself a scholarship and to move on in life.

Noah opened her door.

"Could you knock, please, before you come in?" Ash asked.

He stared at her. He didn't say he was sorry. It didn't seem to register that he shouldn't just barge in whenever he felt like it. "It's your turn to take out the garbage and recycling."

"I did it last week," she protested.

"I said, it's your turn to take out the garbage and recycling." This time there was force in his voice. Ash really hated that voice.

She looked at Noah, her face serious. "I'm doing homework right now."

"As long as it's out by morning. That's all that matters."

With that, he shut the door. He knew how to get the final word on things. He knew how to keep the talk short and get what he wanted. Ash wondered if there was some sort of lesson there for her. Should she learn from him to treat others that way to get what she wanted? The memory of her mom said no. Her heart said no. Noah was horrible.

Ash didn't want to give him the satisfaction of caving in to his request right away. She didn't want it to look like she was at his beck and call, even though she was. She waited for a couple of hours. After midnight, when she knew he'd be asleep, she went down to the garage and hauled out the bins.

In the alley, she sensed activity. A mouse darted across the way. Or was it a rat? Ash stood still for a moment. She didn't want to disturb the little creature's life. Indeed, it wasn't long before the family of rats let themselves be seen. She watched them silently. She admired how they built their world in and amongst people who threw away the stuff they needed. They were survivors. Ash understood them.

Back upstairs, she was about to go to sleep when she checked the app one last time. There were more than a hundred members now and she still hadn't done anything to promote the thing. It was unreal.

Charming was there, wanting to continue their chat.

Charming: Why is it that the further up the mountain you climb, the harder it is to go on?

Cinders: Because the stakes are higher. Farther to fall.

Charming: Yeah, don't I know it?

Cinders: Where are you?

Charming: Nowhere.

Cinders: Cryptic. You some fifty year old dude?

Charming: Nope. Girl. Seventeen.

Cinders: Me too! So you're just being dramatic about your whereabouts?

Charming: Guess so. I'm at home in my room.

Cinders: Cool.

Charming: Not really. What are you still doing up?

Cinders: Chores. Same as always.

Charming: You seem to work a lot.

Cinders: I have big dreams, so I guess don't mind.

Ash thought it was odd that she admitted that. She never talked about her dreams. But what could it hurt to tell some stranger on the Internet? It wasn't like she and Charming would ever meet or anything. Even if the person typing the words was a girl Ash's age, it wasn't like Charming was real. It wasn't like she could be anything more than a fantasy.

Charming: What kinds of dreams?

Cinders: Changing the world. Changing technology.

Charming: Ooooh. Tell me more.

Cinders: I can't. Top secret stuff. You know how it is. ;)

Charming: You secret service?

Cinders: Even worse: high school. But I have a project that might get me the scholarship I need. So I can't take any chances. Sorry. You seem nice though.

Charming: I AM nice.

Cinders: Whoa. Defensive! I believe you.

Charming: It's cool. I can't exactly tell you about my dreams, but I have them too.

Cinders: It's okay to keep your dreams to yourself.

Charming: I guess it is.

Cinders: It's the only way they'll come true. It's the only way they'll survive.

Ash and Charming chatted again the next night. About nothing. About everything. Soon it became a routine and something for Ash to look forward to. It wasn't that Ash stopped missing her mom, or stopped thinking about her. But something about Charming made Ash's heart lighter. Ash began to see that maybe she could go on without her mom. It wasn't living like it was when her mom was alive. But it was getting up every morning, knowing she would be in touch with Charming that night. It was getting through Noah's stupid demands and Mimi's Garbage Girl pics.

06 Being Charmed

Charming: Awake?

Cinders: Always.

Charming: Are you working away as usual?

Cinders: You know me too well.

Charming: Not well enough . . .

Cinders: Well, what are you doing?

Charming: Fantasizing. I'm lonely.

Cinders: What are you fantasizing about?

Charming: You.

Cinders: Me?

Charming: Tell me what you look like. Better yet, send me a photo.

Cinders: How do I know you're not some creepy dude?

Charming: I thought we established that. Didn't you believe me?

Cinders: I believe and don't believe everything online.

Charming: So send me your email address.

Ash sent her email address. Another first. She never gave out her 411 online. But she figured it would prove for sure Charming wasn't some weird male perv. Unless, of course, he was a male perv who'd kidnapped a girl her age and was holding her hostage and forcing her to chat with random strangers online . . . Nah. That was too crazy.

Right away, Ash received a photo of a teen girl playing guitar. Her face was hidden by shadows and what looked like a sweep of dark hair. She was reclined on a bed or couch, with the guitar resting against her, like she was cradling it. There was something sensual about the photo. It looked like the girl cuddled her guitar at night. The skin on her arms was the colour of dark coffee with double cream. Her nails had been painted black but they weren't perfect. They were really short, like she'd used the polish to try to stop herself from biting her nails. Ash zoomed in on the picture. Yeah, Charming had hangnails and dry skin on her hands and the polish was flaking off. There was something rough about her. Ash found herself fascinated.

Ash looked at her own hands, dry from the constant work at the cafeteria and at home. No amount of hand cream could fix the fact that she always had her hands in harsh chemicals and high heat. They had matching hangnails, she and this girl out in cyberspace. And, like Charming, Ash kept her nails short. She wasn't a biter. But she didn't like the way long nails caught on things. *They must make it feel like you have daggers at the ends of your fingers*, she thought. Maybe that was why Mimi went through the whole process of going to the nail salon and getting gels or acrylics put on by specialists.

Ash was lost in the world of the photo. Suddenly she realized she hadn't responded. But now she was getting a voice-only call via FaceTime. It was Charming. Ash waited for less than a second before accepting the call.

"Hello?" Ash answered.

"Is that you, Cinders?" Charming asked. "Or did I just send a picture to an online sex-slave ring?"

"No, it's me."

There was a pause. *I'm such a dork*, Ash thought. *Mimi has that right.* Ash knew she had to say something . . .

The guitar, right. "So, music."

"Yep," said the voice. "I'd let you listen, but I'm shy." The voice sounded like a girl Ash's age. It also sounded a little husky.

"That's fair. Maybe one day."

"Some other day for sure."

Ash started to blush at the promise in that statement. "Cool! I mean, you look cool."

"Yes and no. Just when I think I'm cool, I get the reminders from everyone in the world that I'm not."

"That's what SendLove is for."

"You're telling me. That's why I'm on it."

"Glad you found it."

Charming told Ash about her music. Ash thought she sounded fearless, singing in front of a camera. She tried to picture a face to go with the voice. Even after their chats, it was hard to imagine what kind of life Charming led. But Ash liked seeing her black nails and her jean vest and her arms. She liked thinking about how the app connected them. All her life Ash had met people online. But it was different when it was her own app. It was special.

The school was abuzz. In Ash's homeroom, everyone was busy checking their phones and talking about the Performers' Showcase coming up. Ash couldn't imagine what it would take to get up in front of an audience. She was grateful that her passion was binary code and working things out on a computer, not being a musician or actor. It seemed like a curse to have to chase that sort of life. Ash was saddened by the whole thing. People thought fame was cool, but Ash didn't think so. It had to be lonely getting that kind of attention. She chatted off and on with Charming all day, learning about Charming's fear that her search for recognition made her shallow. Ash was amazed that Charming couldn't see the difference. She knew that Charming just wanted to be heard.

That night, too tired to focus on her homework, Ash searched YouTube for Oprah. Her mom used to love Oprah. Now Ash often found herself looking for things her mom loved. Oprah was like a magical being from far away. She had power and could do stuff for other people. You could count on her to make sense even when the world didn't.

Ash found a clip in which Oprah advised viewers to believe in something greater than themselves. Ash thought about that. It was hard for her to believe in anything. She'd lost both a mother and a father. She was alone and in this strange house. And she had to cope with Noah and Mimi. She had the most uphill battle of anyone she knew. She didn't know people who were worse off than her. Of course there were people like that out there in the world. But not in Sunshine Hills in North Delta. Sometimes Ash felt like all she could do was tread water and not drown. She had to earn her scholarship, had to keep her wits about her. Everyone else at the school was talking about partying. They were enjoying the last few months before grad. They talked about what was trending on social media. They talked about what they used to wear, what they'd wear later, and what they'd never wear. Ash had no time for stuff like that. That was not her life. And it probably never would be.

Ash believed in Oprah, but she didn't think she could follow her advice. Ash didn't believe in Jesus or God. Her faith lay in a different direction. She thought in the here and now, in the real world. She thought in zeros and ones. She believed in science and reason and logic. She believed in working hard. Then again, so did Oprah. Sometimes Ash felt like she was a hamster in one of those plastic wheels. She ran and ran, but got nowhere. She was always exhausted. She always wanted to be further along than she was.

Ash was distracted from her thoughts by a chat notification on her laptop.

Charming: You up?

Cinders: Of course.

Charming: What are you doing?

Cinders: Thinking about what it all means. Hey, let me ask you. What does it all mean?

Charming: Life? Damned if I know. Why are you thinking about that?

Cinders: Because Oprah believes in Jesus and I think she's happier for it. I'm envious.

Charming: My family is Christian, and I can tell you straight up. Don't waste time feeling envy.

Cinders: You're Christian?

Charming: I didn't say that. I said my family is Christian. Well, half my family.

Cinders: But . . . are you?

Charming: You're gonna have to buy me dinner first if you want to know. ;)

Cinders: Ok. When?

Charming: I didn't think you'd actually go for it. You must be having a real crisis of faith.

Cinders: I kind of am. It's just hard to not know anything about where it's all going.

Charming: Christians don't know either. Really.

Cinders: But it's comforting to think about an afterlife, isn't it? I mean . . . Heaven.

Charming: Comforting if you think you'll make the cut. Kind of awful if you think you've already screwed up your chances.

Cinders: I think my parents made the cut.

Charming: Oh. I'm sorry.

Cinders: Thanks.

Charming: When?

Cinders: My dad when I was a kid. My mom a couple of months ago.

Charming: Oh, man.

Cinders: Yeah.

Charming: You want to talk about it?

They did. All night. Ash told Charming about how she felt like she could see her mom everywhere.

Like she had just left the room, or that she was about to walk into the kitchen. It wasn't like seeing a ghost, but like she was really there. And it wasn't spooky. It was comforting.

Ash wished she could have more of that. That was the thing about reality. It could be augmented. Ash thought about stuff like that all the time, how technology could create worlds. Some people her age already lived in video games and their lives were all about being in a virtual world. But what Ash believed was that reality itself didn't need to go anywhere. All it needed was to be made better. Enhanced.

Still, Ash knew she couldn't tell Charming everything. No matter what, she had to keep her guard up. It was best not to trust anyone. But the words just seemed to fly from her fingers, from her lips, whenever she was in contact with Charming. And the words revealed more about Ash than she had ever told anyone except her mom. Ash wondered how she could feel this close to a person who was not her own flesh and blood. And where it would lead.

07 *Fantasy*

CHARMING WAS TRYING to get Ash to FaceTime. Ash had never used her camera with anyone that she had not met in person. That was one of the first lessons of being online. Never show your face to a stranger. Keep your camera covered in case Snowden and all the paranoid people were right. In case hackers and spies could see you through the lens. You can learn from people online. Take tutorials. Make "friends." But never assume you know anyone or what they're up to. Think of the creepiest creep you've ever met and remember that you could be talking to that guy.

Cinders: Not into it. Sorry.

Charming: You're no fun.

Cinders: You're pushy.

Charming: You don't have to show your face. You've seen a picture of me. Let me have something to look at.

Cinders: Fine.

Ash tried to find an angle for her laptop that wouldn't include either her face or a cardboard box. The only one seemed to be straight up at the ceiling. Before she could move her laptop, she got the FaceTime request. When she answered, the small window revealed warm lighting and what looked like a cosy and stylish bedroom.

"Hello, Charming? Where are you?"

"Home. Where else?"

"Your room looks nice."

"More like lonely."

Ash felt weird. How come talking was easier when it was just their voices?

Suddenly Charming asked, "Is that the ceiling?"

"Uh, yes. I couldn't find a view that didn't show me or . . ."

Charming laughed. Ash had come to love the sound of Charming's laugh. "Paranoid much?"

"I'm sorry," Ash said. She was surprised to realize she was. "Trust issues."

"Okay. Does this help?"

Charming took Ash on a tour of her bedroom. Ash compared the fine furniture and art prints on the wall with her own spare bed. *I might as well be living in a storage closet*, thought Ash. But she noticed that the cam was lingering on things like glass animals and well-thumbed books. When the focus turned to the guitar that Ash had seen in the picture, Charming started humming a tune. Ash couldn't place it, but it sounded like all the songs she liked rolled into one.

"What is that?" Ash asked.

"The song?" Charming asked. "Oh, it's just

something I was working on this afternoon. I don't have words for it yet."

"You wrote that?"

"Yeah. You want to hear what I've got so far?"

The frame on Ash's screen settled on a little glass bird. She heard Charming tune a string on the guitar. Then out of her laptop speaker came music.

Ash was still floating on the tune after Charming had stopped playing. At first she barely noticed that Charming had picked up her laptop again. That is, until Charming ran her laptop camera up and down the length of her body. Charming was lying on her bed in a black cotton tank and underwear. The tank was all bunched up around her middle, so there was a lot of skin showing. A lot of smooth, light brown skin that Ash imagined touching. *Stop it*, Ash told herself. It wasn't anything more than you'd see at a sleepover. Not that Ash had ever been to one.

Ash was trying to figure out what to say. But Charming beat her to it.

"So now you've seen everything except my face.

Come on, Cinders, show me something."

I guess that would only be fair, Ash thought. She could tell she was making excuses for her reaction to the seduction in Charming's voice. "What do you want to see?" she asked.

"Everything." Ash could hear the grin in that one word.

Ash blushed. No girl had ever talked to her like that. For that matter, no guy had, either. She thought she might be dreaming, or caught in one of her rare fantasies. But she wasn't. This was happening.

"Do I get to see what I show? I didn't see your legs," said Ash. "How about my legs?"

"Nope," replied Charming. "Not good enough. Do you always negotiate this hard?"

"Fine. Cleavage shot." Ash laughed when she said it. The whole idea of it was absurd.

"Now we're talking. You first."

Ash looked down at herself. "I'll be right back!"

Ash grabbed a cardigan and ran to the bathroom in the hall. She was wearing an oversized t-shirt. She had picked it out of a bin of free stuff at the mall, and it looked like it. It had *Rainbow RV Park — Stay for a week, a month or a year!* printed across her chest. No way could she let Charming see that. Ash took it off and examined herself in the mirror. No one had seen her topless before. Ash threw on the cardigan and did it up, leaving the top few buttons undone.

What am I doing? she wondered as she scooted back to her room. This could very well be the moment her life would derail. Soon everything would go horribly wrong. But she couldn't fight the feeling building inside her. This was the most fun she'd had for as long as she could remember. It was exciting. And there was no way she was talking to some creepy dude. She was talking to a real girl. And not just any girl, either. Someone she liked more than she'd ever liked anyone before.

Wearing the cardigan, Ash propped herself up on her pillows. She pointed the camera at the wall behind her.

"I don't know if I can do this, Charming," she said.

"Of course you can."

Ash squealed. She sounded like she was on a roller coaster ride. And that's what this was. She angled the camera to show her buttoned cardigan. The top button was pulling a bit.

"Nice!" Charming said.

"Yeah?" Ash blushed. The heat of her cheeks was intense. And then it spread through the rest of her. She felt a full body rush at this whole thing. It was so crazy and so unlike her.

"Totally."

Ash laughed. It was far beyond anything she had ever done before. She had heard about stuff like this as she idly listened in on other people's conversations. Mostly, she had been horrified. But now she understood how easy it would be to go too far. It was so much fun.

"You know, that's not a real cleavage shot. Can't you unbutton for me?"

Ash was turned on by the mock sadness in Charming's voice. She had never known this feeling before. Not with a real person causing it. Even though Charming wasn't in the room with her, Ash felt like she was. Even if she had never seen her face, she knew that Charming was real. And so was the way Ash felt about her. As real as anything she'd ever felt before.

"Come on, Cinders," said Charming. "I want to see what's under your sweater."

It was everything Ash had been warned against. And yet she didn't feel unsafe. She wanted to do what Charming told her to do. Despite all her modesty, despite her lack of experience, she flashed the camera.

Then a wave of anxiety came over her. She wanted to curl up into a little ball and disappear. But she also wanted to spread her arms as wide as they would go. She wanted to jump up and down as though she'd come first in a race.

"Hey," Charming said. "That was brave."

Ash giggled. "I can't believe I did that. You didn't grab a screen shot, did you?"

"Of course not. Don't you trust me?"

"Well . . ."

"You will. I'll prove to you that you can."

Ash heard a knock at a door. Charming's door. A

voice told her to go to sleep and Charming said she would.

"Sorry, Cinders," Charming said. "I gotta get going. Thanks for flashing me."

Ash felt a pang of loss. She had never felt so brazen before. She wasn't quite ready to be on her own again. But Ash had work to do.

"Don't be sorry about anything. You rule, Charming."

"I do?"

"Yep."

Just like that, Ash was cut off from that world. She looked at herself in the mirror. There she was, alone in her room. *What got into me?* she wondered. It was dangerous, this thing she had with a girl she barely knew. It was not what Ash's life was supposed to look like.

But Ash knew there was no way back from the truth. She was queer. She had a crush on Charming and that was that.

08 Back to Reality

ASH WENT TO SCHOOL and tried to forget about her secret fantasy life. People did weird stuff online all the time, right? It didn't mean anything. Or it didn't have to. She focused on her teachers. On learning. She had to nail the year-end project. It was her one shot at a better life. Ash felt like she was running to catch a moving train. She was determined to get on it, even if she had to defy all laws of motion and gravity and velocity to do it. She'd hurl herself at this chance.

She was doing homework in her room when her belly rumbled. She realized she was starving. Ash stopped outside the kitchen. Mimi and her friends were there. Ash squeezed by to get to the fridge. Mimi looked up to see where Ash was going. When she saw that Ash wasn't going anywhere near the garbage, she acted like Ash wasn't there.

"Ugh. So it's so obvious that Char and Everett are a thing now." Mimi stared at her phone. "How pathetic. As if her mom and dad calling themselves the 'King and Queen of Real Estate' means she's even worth noticing."

Mimi's gang rushed to agree with her. Ash thought that Mimi considered Char a friend. Of course, Mimi had also bad-mouthed everyone present. Clearly, her idea of friendship wasn't anything that Ash understood.

"He's kind of hot."

"Yeah, and she's okay. I mean, if you like *that* look," said Janice.

"You think so?" said Mimi, raising her eyebrows.

Suddenly the girls all made scoffing noises.

"Oh, she just wants attention."

"He's way out of her league," one girl said. "I'm pretty sure she's queer."

"What? No way. Why would she be going out with Everett then?"

"Um," said Mimi. "Because he's been in love with her since, like grade eight? She's so full of herself."

"Yeah. Using him because he gives her attention."

"She's awful."

Ash had learned mostly to tune out Mimi and her friends tearing people apart. None of their comments were based on truth as far as Ash could tell. But that was Mimi for you. Shallow and awful. Her friends clearly liked that about her. Except for one girl who kept her head down. *Alice? No, Alison,* Ash thought.

Apple in hand, Ash walked by the group. She didn't make eye contact. But Alison looked up. She stared right at Ash, her dark eyes holding a bit of warmth, and said hi.

Ash panicked a bit. She tried so hard to go unnoticed. It was the only way to survive. But Alison's greeting seemed sincere. Ash returned it with a slight wave. She slinked into her room and went back to her math homework.

Charming didn't reach out that night. Neither did Ash.

Saturday morning, Ash woke feeling lonelier than she had in weeks. She recalled how her mom had loved making brunch on weekends. Inspired, and thinking how long the weekend stretched out before her, she went downstairs. She put on some Ed Sheeran, because her mom had known a bunch of his lyrics and had insisted on singing them even though she was a terrible singer. No one was up yet. Ash got out a mixing bowl, flour, eggs, baking powder, and everything she needed to make muffins. She grated carrots and chopped an apple up. She chopped some walnuts. She fitted paper muffin cups into the pan and scooped the thick batter into each, just like her mom had. She noticed that her hands looked like her mom's. She started licking batter off the wooden spoon. Ash was so caught up in the moment, she almost didn't notice when Ted came in.

"Baking, eh?" he said. He poured some coffee from the machine that was set on a timer to brew even on weekends.

She nodded.

"Your mom would be proud of you," he said.

"Thanks," she said. Ash's mind flashed back to everything that she had done that night with Charming. Maybe baking could be a way to try to recapture her innocence. But no matter how many muffins she churned out, she would not be able to go back to a time before she flashed Charming. Now that the moment was in the past, she felt like she'd put herself on display. She had seen girls do that sort of thing in movies sometimes. They acted flirty with each other, but usually it was because there were boys around. They did it to impress the boys or each other. That wasn't what that night had been for Ash. That had been just about Ash and Charming. Two girls connecting. *Like that.*

The timer jolted Ash back to reality. She took the muffins out of the oven and placed them on a cooling rack. The moment was over. As if he'd been summoned, Noah came groggily into the kitchen and took two muffins. He didn't ask. He didn't say thank you. He just put two of Ash's muffins on a plate and walked past her into the TV room. He turned on golf and slouched into the leather sofa. He ate the muffins.

Ash wanted to believe that somewhere in there Noah had a heart. That he remembered her mom's brunches. That he noticed she had tried to copy the recipe. She wanted to believe that his silence was only because he didn't know the right words to say. Because no words would make it okay. But she watched him chewing and knew she was being too generous.

That night, Ash was in bed, her laptop in front of her, when Charming's name popped up.

Charming: Can we FaceTime?

Ash's mood had been down all day. She hoped that the flirtation of their last session hadn't changed the way Charming felt about her. What she needed was the girl she could tell anything to. But when they connected, she didn't know what to say.

"Cinders, about the other night," Charming started. She sounded serious. Ash was relieved that Charming wasn't casual about it. "I'm sorry if I pushed you. You know, to do things maybe you felt bad about later."

Ash had very much enjoyed it. But she didn't think she could say that. It didn't feel right to admit it. "No, no, Charming. It's fine. You didn't make me do anything I didn't want to do."

"I've been stupid and it's come back to haunt me. It's also been the secret of my success. But I wanted to make sure I didn't hurt you."

"You didn't," Ash said.

What Ash couldn't say was that she would have done more if Charming had asked. She had pushed herself as much as Charming had pushed her that night.

And something inside of her had awoken.

But as they talked, Ash could hear that Charming was troubled. Charming told her how she feared she was as shallow as people thought she was. Ash's heart went out to this girl. How could Charming worry about comparing herself to others and coming up short? Didn't Charming know that Ash could see into her depths? Ash knew what a good and brave person Charming was.

When Charming told Ash that she was planning to unplug for a week, Ash's first thought was that it would be good for Charming. It was only a moment later that Ash wondered if it was to break things off with her. But Ash had to trust that good and brave heart that she knew deep down lived in Charming.

"I'm used to us talking every night," said Ash. "I really kind of love it." She hoped she slipped in the word so that Charming might not even notice it.

"I love it, too," replied Charming.

"It's weird isn't it? How we can feel this way without ever having met?"

"Yeah. It's weird. But I don't question it. I think when the time is right, we will meet."

"I'm scared to meet you," confessed Ash. "What if you don't like me?"

"But I already like you."

"But what if I disappoint you?"

"No way that can happen."

"I'm really going to miss you," sighed Ash.

"It's going to be a long week without you, Cinders."

Ash was in tears.

09 Future Vision

"HOW'D YOU LEARN ABOUT THIS?" Noah asked, scanning the code Ash had worked up. "I thought they only taught that at boot camp."

"There's all kinds of stuff online," Ash said.

"Where?"

She sighed. It bothered her that he wanted her to show him exactly where. He had the advantage already. Why did he need her to show him anything? But she pulled up Katrina's tutorial, all the time berating herself for being too nice.

An ad played. It was one of the ones that lasted sixteen seconds, so it seemed like forever.

"I hate that we have to go through this to get to a two-minute clip," Ash said.

"That's the future," Noah said. He spoke as if he knew everything that was going to happen.

"It doesn't have to be."

"But it will be." So now Noah was an expert. It offended Ash that he thought that way.

"There's still a chance for the free web," she offered.

"Get real. It's only going to get worse once Google Glass and that type of thing catches on."

"Scary thought." Ash dreaded the future Noah saw. She feared a reality where corporate interest controlled the way people moved through the world.

"People have the right to make money."

"Within reason," Ash objected.

Noah shrugged. "That's the way of the world. Greed is good. All that shit."

"Sure. To a degree. But what about corporations

taking advantage of people's addictions and weaknesses? Like targeting you with an ad for your favourite ice cream right when you're walking by the shop. Or worse, after you've been dumped and you're walking by the shop."

"Hey, now that's a good idea!"

"Noah, I'm serious. It's a horrible idea."

"I'm serious, too. There's a great project in there somewhere. Amp it up, though. Tell potheads when they're close to a weed shop. Let alcoholics know where the nearest liquor store is. Better yet, send smokers ads with smoking triggers built in. Why not?"

"Uh, because ethics."

"No, you said it yourself. People have weaknesses. Whose fault is that?"

Ash didn't know how to answer. Sometimes with Noah words were useless. It was like they weren't even speaking the same language. He insisted on twisting her words and thoughts to fit his idea of the way the world worked, or should work. And even though she thought he was dead wrong, she knew it was a losing battle to try to change his mind.

"Anyway," said Noah. "Thanks for the great idea for the final project. I hope you didn't want to use it for your own. It's mine now."

Ash just stared at him. Her mind refused to process what he was saying.

"At first I thought I should do some kind of girl-rating app. But it's way better to do something that exploits addictions and cravings."

"I don't even know what to say." Ash really wanted no part in it. She could barely believe what she was hearing.

"Don't get me wrong. I'll be passing off the grunt work to you. But there's a whole lot going on up here." He tapped his forehead with his index finger. "The vision is the important part."

After he left, Ash realized that the only good thing that had come out of talking with Noah was that he wasn't going to develop the girl-rating app. She knew that it would give guys like Noah the power to prey on girls' self-esteem. Rating girls wasn't a thing at her school that she was aware of. Of course, Ash wouldn't be the sort to know about it. No one would be interested enough to rate her, and that was something she was grateful for. It would be a nightmare for the girls who obsessed about their weight and wanted their parents' permission to have plastic surgery underage. Even the girls who did their makeup between classes and posted selfies to public accounts to collect as many hearts as possible. All of it made her think about Mimi and how she would, in her own way, be into that sort of thing as long as she was being validated. Ash thought about what Mimi would do with that sort of app at her disposal. The thought was terrifying.

But was the idea Noah had twisted out of Ash's words any better? Ash knew that one day Noah could easily be working for Google. He'd be able to put his addiction-fuelled ad schemes into action. And he'd get paid boatloads of money for it, too.

If that was the world she'd have to live in, Ash wanted out. But she was already in too deep. She couldn't go live in a cabin in the woods. It wasn't like she knew anything about that sort of survival. No, her world, like Noah's, was a virtual one. But she wanted something else from online culture. She wanted culture. Safety. Compassion. The Internet was still like the Wild West. Anything could happen. Jerks like Noah could win out. But, maybe, just maybe, Ash could be the new sheriff in town.

Up in her room, Ash went through videos she had of her mom and dad. She watched, over and over, a blurry clip of her dad tucking in a tiny Ash one night. Her mom is holding the camera. Her dad looks at her mom and says, "I can't believe she's ours. She's so beautiful."

Ash could see that her mom is nodding and even hear her crying. Ash thought about how she would give anything to have a moment like that now. If she could only feel her mom's love. She scrolled through more recent footage and found a clip of Ash and her mom doing their dance routine to "Gangnam Style." It was cute the way her mom moved just like Psy in the video. It made Ash laugh, even though she was really crying. On the screen of Ash's laptop, her mom was still alive, dancing and loving Ash.

Ash missed her mom so much. Life would be a

million times better if she could see her mom. And why not? You had to live with images of ice cream and expensive shoes and all the things companies wanted you to buy. Surely you should be able to preserve the people you loved.

Why couldn't augmented reality be used to really add to reality? To add back the people who had gone? To add beauty and music and love? Ash's mind raced. This would be her year-end project. It would be the reverse of Noah's project, the cure. And Noah would never know that Ash would be using his project to get her own done. The coding would be the same.

The difference between a hopeful future and a bleak one was clear. And it rested squarely on Ash's shoulders as she tapped away on her keyboard. The old cord snaked across her bed, its wires nearly exposed. One day she'd have a better laptop and she'd be able to do so much more. But for now, she was riding into the great Wild West on a tired old pony. Alone.

By the time a week without Charming had passed, Ash couldn't wait to hear from her. At the same time, she knew she wouldn't have time to talk to Charming late into the night, every night. She was moderating as many SendLove discussion boards as she could. She still had work at the cafeteria and chores at home. The school showcase was coming up. Ash would make extra money working extra hours that evening. But it was that much time taken from her work on her augmented reality project. How could Charming understand how important the project was to Ash? That the only chance Ash would have to deserve Charming was to get out of Delta and start her own life?

Ash saw the FaceTime call finally come, but didn't answer. It wasn't until she knew what she had to do that she called Charming back.

"I've been thinking about you," Charming said as soon as she answered. "About us."

"You have?" Ash started melting at the sound of her voice. But then she steeled herself. Maybe Charming had decided that she didn't have time for Ash, too.

"Yeah. Like a lot."

"I've been thinking, too," Ash said. If this was the big brush-off, Ash could beat Charming to it. "Here's the thing. I need to focus. I have so much going on right now. So much work and school."

"Me too. I'm busy, too," Charming said.

So that was it. It would be the best in the long run. Ash cared about Charming. She knew that the last thing Charming wanted in her life was a Garbage Girl.

10 Garbage Girl

ASH FINISHED THE STACK of dishes at the cafeteria. Her hands were nicked and her skin was rough from using steel wool on the pots and pans. Alfredo sauce was the worst, the way it stuck to the bottom and formed a light brown layer you had to scrape off. The only good part was that her shift was over. She took a garbage bag down to the recycling room and went through the bins, collecting the returnable cans and bottles. Once she had a full bag, she tied a knot to close it and slung it over her shoulder. She was like the world's saddest Santa.

Ash put her backpack on her other shoulder and walked out of the school, into the rain. Since it was only a few blocks to the recycling depot, she'd save herself bus fare and the hassle of managing such a big bag on the bus. She was walking along, her head in her own world. Then she felt a tug at her back. She heard the sound of falling cans and bottles. She turned and saw a Jeep speed away. A hand with a cellphone pointed at her stuck out of one window and a field hockey stick stuck out of another. They must have used the stick to tear the bag at the bottom, because the cans and bottles had spilled out into the street and all around Ash. She was still holding the top of the bag. It was just a mess.

It was hard to tell for sure who was in the car. But the long flowy hair was recognizable. Mimi. It had to be.

What fun could it possibly be to pick on such an easy target? Ash didn't try to compete with Mimi and her friends. All she wanted was to fly under the radar, to be totally ignored by the likes of them. Was that too much to ask?

Ash was drenched with rain. She was cold. Her hands were freezing. She tied the end of the trash bag together. It made the bag much smaller and all the bottles wouldn't fit. So she jammed some of them into her backpack. She was scared that the wetness would ruin her laptop. But what could she do? She couldn't just leave them in the street for other people to have to deal with.

By the time Ash got to the recycling depot just off Scott Road, she felt like a sewer rat. The clerk took her bag. She tallied up some coins and handed Ash a fistful of change. "Three dollars and sixty cents."

Ash took the money and said thank you.

Mimi was primping and preening with her friends in her giant bathroom. Everyone was talking outfits and boys and lash extensions and hairspray. Ash crept quietly into her room.

She wanted not to look at Mimi's Instagram account. But she'd have to face the music sooner or later. She hated that by just hovering over the video, she was adding to the view count. It would be easier if she could just ignore it. But how was she supposed to do that?

There she was, the sad portrait of a mousy teen girl. Her short, stringy hair was weighed down by rain. Her thin plaid shirt was sticking to her. Her ball cap did nothing to obscure her face. The splash of bottles and cans looked like a person's intestines pouring out. The look of pain on her face as she turned toward the camera was pathetic. But Ash needed to keep collecting those bottles and cans. Every dollar mattered. With each drop off at the recycling depot, Ash was one step closer to leaving Delta for good. That might seem stupid to Mimi and girls like her, but they had parents who footed bills. They had homes they could stay in after graduation. They had all kinds of things that Ash did not.

Beneath the photo were already some laughing emojis and some LOLs. Soon everyone would know that Ash collected bottles and cans for recycling. She might as well spend the rest of high school with a paper bag over her face. Ash would have loved to lie low until it went away. But tonight was the Performers' Showcase at school. Her boss would be totally screwed without her. If Ash didn't show, she might get fired. As lousy as the job was, it was the best thing Ash had. Her best shot at getting away next year. No, there was no way out. She had to go.

She looked through her wardrobe and picked a drab sweater to go with her plain Old Navy jeans. She was almost out the door when Ted came out to the foyer.

As Mimi and her crew came down the stairs, they gave off the scent of the fragrance counter at The Bay.

"You guys are giving Ash a lift to school, aren't you?" Ted asked.

Mimi looked stunned. "Uh . . ."

"I'm okay," Ash said.

"How are you getting there?" Ted asked.

"Bus?" Ash said.

One of Mimi's friends snickered. Mimi elbowed her.

Alison said, "We should take her."

Mimi sneered at Alison.

Alison said, "What? We're all going to the same place. What's the problem?"

Ted looked at Ash with pity. He said, "I'll give you a lift. I know Noah would do it but he already left."

"It's really fine," Ash said. Couldn't Ted see that his kindness was just making things worse? Ash was so alone in the world that it was better to be really and truly alone. No pretending.

"We'll take her," Mimi said.

Alison smiled.

"Oh, it's okay. Really," Ash protested. "I'll take the bus. It's cool."

"You'd rather go to school by bus than in my Mercedes?" Mimi said.

Ash wanted to nod. If someone nice had offered to take her in a rusty old bathtub on wheels, she'd have accepted. It wasn't the car. It was the company.

"Well, hurry up and get changed," ordered Mimi. "We leave in ten."

"I'm ready any time."

"You're wearing *that*?" one of Mimi's friends shrieked.

"It's not that bad," said Alison. "But I'm sure we can find something better."

"It really doesn't matter," Ash said. "I'm working."

"Seriously, I have a cute dress you can borrow," said Alison. She held out an orange dress that set off her own dark skin perfectly. Ash knew that, with her pale skin, the colour would make her look like one of the dishrags she used at work. Alison started digging in her bag. "And I have an extra pair of earrings. At least borrow some makeup."

"It's really okay," Ash said. "I wouldn't want to lose your earrings. And the dress would get dirty. I mean, that's what happens when you work at the cafeteria. And take bottles to recycle." She threw in the last part just to see if they'd look guilty. And they did. It wasn't like Ash could or would do anything about it, but at least she knew the truth.

Mimi and her friends looked horrified. Like it was the worst fate in the world to make money by having an actual job. Ash paid them no mind. She just didn't care.

"Okay, well, I guess we can go any time, then," Mimi said. She gave Ted a hug and said, "Enjoy your evening."

"Have a good one, Sweetie," he said.

Ash found it sickening that Ted couldn't see how horrible his daughter was. But she couldn't fault him for it. Ted and Mimi were flesh and blood after all. Ted was a decent human being. It was weird that he had such awful kids.

11 A Night Out

GETTING OUT OF MIMI'S CAR, Ash thought they looked like stars at a red carpet event. Only Ash was more like the star's dog walker or shoe shiner.

"Catch you later," Ash said to no one in particular as she strode off. Out of habit, she checked her phone. Charming was back online. Ash had decided that she'd been ghosted. She figured Charming had lost interest and wasn't going to message or FaceTime her ever again.

When Ash got to work, the cafeteria was set up to highlight the students trying to get into arts programs. There was a stage set up and a video camera to tape performances. It didn't even smell like the cafeteria. There was a buzz in the air. There were possibilities. This was the sort of place where romantic connections happened. Maybe not for Ash, but for others. For Ash, all it meant was an extra shift.

"Good. You're here. Hurry up and grab those flats," Sally said.

Each heavy flat was a tray of twenty-four cans of soft drinks. By the time Ash had hauled them from the storage pantry to the big ice buckets she'd be selling them out of, she was sweating. She had to count her float. She set up a menu board. People were already piling in.

Ash could see that Sally was stressed out. "Okay, we need the candy rack to move. We still have to get the sandwiches into the display fridges." She clapped her hands in Ash's direction. "Chop, chop!"

"Okay, I'm on it!" Ash wasn't one to twiddle

her thumbs. But she really felt pumped. Suddenly she wished she wasn't wearing the drab sweater. She wished she'd taken Alison up on the offer of a dress, even though Ash didn't like wearing dresses.

She was still running around when a line started to form.

"Get me a couple of waters and a bag of chips," ordered one guy. Ash had seen him in Math class, but she didn't know his name.

"I'll take a Vitamin Water," said the next person in line.

On and on it went. Ash thought she'd get her usual fifteen-minute breaks. But it soon became clear that she couldn't leave the counter. Sally didn't need to say anything. The look she gave Ash was enough.

Ash had barely had a chance to even look at the stage when the music started. It felt like everyone from school was there. They all wanted some sort of pop or snack from her.

Ash was in the flow. She was alone managing the drinks and candy. But it was going pretty well. She was into the music, nodding along. She had a good pace going. Then one of the ice buckets, mostly filled with water now that the ice had melted, was tilted in her direction. Bottles went everywhere. Freezing cold water splashed all over Ash. She felt her front get drenched. And there she was in a white t-shirt that was now wet and see-through. Right in front of her was a phone, recording it all.

Ash didn't flinch. She didn't even skip a beat. She kept serving. Then it hit her that it was not an accident. It had to have been a set up. Why was someone taking video with their phone in the snack line? She put up the emergency "Back in five" sign they kept in the bottom of the cash drawer. Sally had told her not to use it unless it was life or death. To Ash, it felt like that.

Ash went to her locker to get her gym clothes. A hideous team shirt was better than a see-through wet shirt any day. As she changed in the washroom, something in her broke. She was tired of trying to tough it out on her own. She was tired of waiting for Charming to come back and rescue her from her own thoughts. For the first time, she turned to SendLove. She opened the app and posted that she'd been set up and recorded earlier that day with the bottles. She wrote that any second there'd be another upload of her getting drenched.

Without contact with Charming, Ash had been trying to train herself not to check her phone so much. But now she couldn't help sneaking a quick peek. Her mom had told her it was the worst part about life now. Everyone was attached to their phones instead of really connecting. All she and Charming ever had was what happened on screens and phones. Thinking about that, Ash felt a sense of loneliness set in. She put her phone away.

Now that she was back in action in front of her cash register, Ash was alert. She looked at everyone with new eyes. Her shirt was dry and her trust level low. All these people could be out to get her for all she knew. Ash didn't want to believe that the world was cruel, but the proof was all around her. She listened to the music that came from the stage. Something about it made Ash feel like she'd been born in the wrong place or at the wrong time.

A break in the music was a relief to Ash. She saw Char Gill, the girl that Mimi pretended to like but really hated, step up on the stage. *She walks like a warrior*, Ash thought. When the girl nodded to the audience, Ash could swear she was included in the welcome. The girl grabbed her guitar and sat on a stool. Ash saw the music teacher signal to one of the dudes on a high platform to change the lights. The switch to warm incandescent bulbs turned the mood to intimate. A spotlight shone on the girl with the guitar. And then she sang.

Ash, who had been catching moments of the show by stealing glances, stopped what she was doing and stared. The music was beautiful. Breathtaking. Char Gill sang about love and connection. She sang about a love that had captured her heart. Ash felt that the words and the voice were speaking directly to her own heart.

"Can I get a kombucha?" someone asked. But Ash didn't hear. She was so lost in the song that Sally had to give her a shove.

Ash had always thought Char Gill was like Mimi, but not as mean. But it was clear that Char Gill was singing a love song to a girl. It was the bravest thing Ash had ever seen. Ash and this girl both were caught in this den of conformity. They were surrounded by the type of people who would throw ice water on someone just so they could film it and put it online. But this girl was boldly telling everyone that she was different. No matter who you were or how cool, at this school you wanted to keep any and all differences on the down low. So Ash was shocked when the crowd cheered. Ash surprised herself by screaming out. She usually stayed quiet, kept out of sight. But she had to voice her support for someone who dared to be different. Sally snapped her fingers in front of Ash's face. Back on planet Earth, Ash tied up bags of cans and bottles. She left them in the back of the cafeteria to be picked up later. When she got back to the snack bar, the first person in line was Char Gill.

Ash kept her head down as she got the sandwich Char ordered from the case. When she looked up, she saw something like recognition in Char's eyes. Ash had to say something in answer to that kindness.

"I heard your song." Ash spoke softly, hoping that the noise in the cafeteria would drown her out. "It was amazing."

The girl surprised Ash by asking, "It really sounded okay?" The hope in her eyes made it clear she wasn't asking just to get more praise. She seemed really pleased by Ash's comment. So Ash confessed that she had had to stop working and listen during the song.

"You were great," Ash said. She wished she could think of something clever to say. But she was having a hard time talking. Her heart pounded in her chest and she wanted to run. Now that Ash knew she liked girls, was she going to fall for every girl who smiled at her?

12 *Creation*

WHEN ASH GOT HOME, she checked Dorks of North Delta. There they were. Two Garbage Girl videos in one day. That had to be a record. But what was more interesting than her own embarrassment was the way SendLove people came to her rescue. Everyone was all hearts. They drowned out the voices of the mean people.

Only jerks post stuff like this.
Awww. Poor thing. She seems nice.

Mean people suck.

Ash didn't like the feeling of being a lab rat in a science experiment of her own creation. But it was neat to see that the app was working. Ash sat in her room and thought about all the other cool people out there. Maybe, like her, they were alone, or felt alone. But together they were strong. Together they made bullying less fun for whoever was doing it. In a way, Ash was glad she had been a target so she could see SendLove from the other side. It let her see that it could have been anyone. It wasn't personal. It wasn't anyone picking up on anything about her. She once heard Maya Angelou talking about protecting a place inside yourself that can never be touched. That place inside of Ash was still safe. That place didn't get wet, didn't get spilled on. It didn't get captured on camera because it wasn't visible to anyone. It was hers alone. And SendLove was helping keep that space safe for every member.

The SendLove community had become so big that Ash couldn't handle all the traffic herself. She couldn't follow every person being targeted. But members had stepped up. She was surprised at how many of them had started moderating discussion boards. She noted that each one seemed to want to focus on the topic and cases that meant the most to them. But it was hard for them to follow one member, or to group together one kind of online bullying. Ash could fix that. She could make it so that SendLove would be easier to navigate for everyone, no matter how much or little they wanted to be involved. She could make it easier to forge real online connections. Maybe even real online friendships.

Ash saw that Charming was online. She minimized the chat window so she wouldn't have to see her little green light. It was a relief that Charming was still using the app. Ash still thought about Charming a lot, but they hadn't been in touch. So it surprised her when Charming messaged her, asking to FaceTime. Ash felt a rush of pleasure as she opened a new window and called Charming.

"Where've you been hiding?" Charming asked.

"I've been around," Ash said.

"Are you mad at me?"

"Why would I be mad at you?"

"I figured maybe you were done with me."

"Just the opposite," Ash said. "Actually, I think about you so much that it makes it hard to work sometimes."

"Then we should be connecting," Charming said. "Because my life is so much better with you in it."

Ash didn't know how to reply to that. She wanted to tell Charming how much bigger her own life was with Charming in it. Ash wanted to say that she'd never felt for anyone the attraction she felt to Charming. She wanted to admit to herself that she was already half in love with Charming. But what could Ash offer a girl like that? "I see you're sending love, too," said Ash finally.

"Oh? You're on SendLove right now?"

"I'm always on it," Ash said, smiling.

"Yeah, I've noticed you're pretty active. It's cool,"

Charming said. "But it makes me wonder about all this work you claim to be doing."

"What can I say?"

"Are you okay with us being forever on opposite sides of a screen? Is there ever going to be a time when we could meet for real?"

Ash's heart beat faster at the very idea of meeting Charming. But it wouldn't work. It couldn't work. "I can't."

"Just like that?" Charming asked. "You're breaking my heart here."

"I'm sorry," Ash said. "Maybe we shouldn't be FaceTiming anymore. It's not you. It's my crazy life. I have so much I need to get done."

"Yet you're spending all this time on an app."

"Well, yeah. I'm working out the kinks."

"You work for SendLove?"

"I created SendLove."

"You whaaaaa??? What do you mean you created it? Isn't it like a totally big and legit thing?"

"It is to me."

"Aren't you in high school like me? Am I talking to some thirty-year-old Silicon Valley lady?"

"No, no. I'm in high school. It's part of my coding class."

"Shut up. You did this for school?"

"For extra credit. But yeah."

"Holy shit, girl. For real?"

"Yeah, for real."

"Why the hell didn't you tell me sooner?"

"I don't know. It never came up."

"Never came up? Are you kidding me? If I had created something like that, I'd be telling everyone I know."

"We're different, you and I." Ash smiled. It felt good that Charming was impressed with her.

"I'll say! I can't believe you. I mean, I really can't believe you. Are you even real?"

"Of course I'm real. I'm sitting here talking to you, aren't I?" Ash asked. "And you can hear me typing as well. That's me trying to work out a kink."

"So that's why you're always on the app."

"Of course. I'm the admin."

"God, I feel like I'm talking to a star or something."

"Don't overdo it, Charming. I'll feel like you're making fun of me."

"I'm not making fun of you. I'm in awe of you."

"It's not that big a deal," Ash said.

"Not that big a deal? Are you kidding me? You're giving people an antidote to bullying. That is so friggin' huge."

"I guess so."

"Cinders. It is."

Just as Charming said she had go to the bathroom, Noah burst into Ash's room.

Ash looked up from her laptop. "Want to knock next time?"

She wished could be more blunt. "Knock, jerk!" would have been better. But she didn't like talking that way. Not even to Noah. Her mom had raised her better than that.

"You have to help me," whined Noah. "This code is just killing me." He threw his brand new MacBook

Pro at her. "I've been trying for two whole hours and it's not working."

Ash often spent days making something work. It was all about going through the code bit by bit, looking for such little things as a period out of place. It took the kind of care that someone like Noah just didn't have.

"What are you working on?" Noah demanded.

"Something for extra credit," Ash replied. There was no way she would let Noah know about SendLove. She knew he would laugh at it. Worse, he would look for a way to ruin it.

Ash took Noah's computer onto her lap and sighed. She tried to make sense of what she saw. "Let me look," she said. "Give me some time."

"Perfect," said Noah. "I'm gonna go grab a snack."

13 Breaking Off

BY THE TIME CHARMING came back, Ash had worked out a new organizing map for SendLove and was looking at Noah's work.

"I should get going," Ash said.

She didn't think she could bear hearing about Charming's retreat. Not when Ash didn't even have a room she could really call her own.

"Wait. I really missed you. I was sort of looking forward to connecting again. I missed our talks,"

Charming said.

"Really?" Ash hadn't even admitted to herself how much she missed Charming. How much she wanted something to prove that she wasn't alone. That she wasn't the only one having really intense feelings.

"Totally."

"What actually is this thing we have?" Ash asked suddenly.

She had never been that bold before. Unsure of where it came from, Ash savoured the feeling. It was good to ask questions. It was good to put her own truth out there.

"I'm not sure," Charming said. "I think about you all the time."

"Do you have another girlfriend? Or anything I should know about?"

"I often get asked if I have a boyfriend, but only because my best friend is a guy. We're super close. But it's not like that."

"Not like what?" Ash knew she sounded like a stalker. She sounded possessive.

"Not like this. I told him about you."

"You did?" Ash wanted to cry. She didn't know why. It was important to be brave. And Charming was being totally brave.

"Well, sure. Haven't you told anyone about me?"

"Actually, no." Ash felt bad that she hadn't. Who would she tell? "But that's because I don't really have anyone to tell."

"Friends at school?"

"I guess I'm just private. I don't mind when people tell me stuff. But I don't usually talk too much. It's pretty rare for me to meet anyone I trust and like."

"So you're saying you like me?" Charming asked.

Ash blushed. She was glad that her face wasn't visible. She touched her cheeks with her hands. They were hot. "I guess that's what I'm saying."

"I'm glad." Charming's voice was deep. "Yeah, I told my guy friend about how we have this intense connection even though we've never met in real life. He said, 'What are you waiting for? Meet up!' But then I told him that I'm scared to."

Ash nodded to her laptop. She understood the fear. Now she wished that Charming could see her so she'd know Ash was nodding, agreeing with her, surprised to hear that Charming, who was otherwise so bold, was conflicted like her. "What are you afraid of?" Ash asked.

"Honestly, I'm afraid of what happens next. I'm not sure I'm ready. I'm trying to build a life for myself. I'm not sure where a relationship fits into that. Especially with a girl."

"Is your family homophobic?" Ash asked.

"Kind of. Not toward other people. But it'd be a problem if *their* daughter came out."

"Maybe you just need to give them time and space to understand it?"

"You don't know my family."

"No, but I do know what it's like to be around people who aren't nice to you."

"My family likes to project a perfect image," Charming said. "Great house, great neighbourhood, well-balanced kids who are doing what they love."

"Yeah," said Ash sadly. "I don't have any of that.

But I can see how it'd be hard in its own way."

"I don't think it's easier being you, I hope you didn't get that sense."

"Not at all. For the record, my mom was really open-minded. I think she would have been excited to meet you," Ash said.

"So, um, would you want to meet?" asked Charming.

"I'm scared, too," Ash said.

"Of what?" Charming wanted to know.

"Of you seeing what my life is like." There. She said it. She didn't have to give details.

"What do you mean?"

"Well, I work hard. I'm kind of a nerd. But more than that. I don't have a life."

"I don't either."

"I know that's not true." Ash said. She could sense that Charming had way more going on than Ash did in terms of a social life. "I have so much I have to do this year. Everything is riding on these next few months. My entire future. I can't really afford to get distracted."

"You really keep your head down, don't you?"

"Yep. I realized the other night when I was taking out the trash that I feel like the rats in the alley. They're just trying to get by, do their thing, and go unnoticed. In fact, the secret to their survival is going unnoticed."

"Huh. I think it's been the opposite for me. I've made myself very visible. Because there's power in that."

It felt so wonderful to Ash that she and Charming were talking again that she let the conversation go on. Words and feelings swirled around her. She felt like she could live inside the sound of Charming's voice. She found she was only half paying attention to what they were actually saying. They were finally telling each other where they lived. Ash figured it wouldn't be a bad thing. She wanted to be able to have more specific fantasies about Charming. But then she was shocked out of her daze.

Did Ash just confirm to Charming that they both lived in Delta? That they both went to Seaquam?

Ash started getting anxious. Who could Charming be? Ash realized she didn't know anyone at school except for Noah, Mimi, and their friends. Was this just another way for Mimi to make a fool of Ash? Part of Ash knew that Mimi just wasn't smart enough to plan something like this. But if Charming wasn't Mimi or one of her friends setting up Ash, then she was real. And Ash couldn't think of a single person at her school who would even talk to the school's Garbage Girl. Much less be seen with her.

"We have to meet," Charming said.

"Um. I don't know." Ash tried to sound calm. But she was in full-out panic mode now. She wondered what would happen if she just never went back to school. That way Charming would never find her.

"For real? All this stuff in common. And this weird cosmic connection we have. And you don't know if you want to meet up?"

"I'm shy?"

"What are you afraid of?"

"Honestly? Everything." At least that was the truth.

"Yeah. I get that. Me, too."

"Really? Because you don't seem afraid."

"Are you kidding me?"

"You don't. You seem kind of fearless."

"Well, I'm not."

"I don't know. It's worse that we're at the same school. I don't like who I am at school. Or who I've been made out to be."

Ash meant to shut down the call. She really did. But somehow Charming got her to calm down. She got her talking about her year-end project. She told Charming about using augmented reality to bring her mother back into her life. And that was when Ash realized she could never let Charming be part of her life, not even a little. For Charming's sake.

Ash tried to let Charming down easy. And then she shut down her laptop and cried.

14 Making It Work

ASH THOUGHT ABOUT NOAH and Mimi and the kind of space they took up, simply by being visible. They got noticed and they seemed happy with it. They even craved it. Ash always thought people like that were jerks. Sadly, Ash thought about what Charming had said about the power in being visible. Charming had made Ash rethink everything.

Noah was watching TV in the living room when Ash came downstairs before school. She watched him.

She saw the way he stared blankly at the screen while the ads were on.

"Hey, Noah," she said. "Do you really want to live in a world where it's nothing but ads all the time?"

He looked at her like she was speaking a different language. A cereal ad came on. Ash recognized the jingle from when she was a little kid. Noah hummed the tune and laughed. Then he shrugged and said, "Whatever."

"It really doesn't bother you at all, does it?"

"Why are you still so worked up about this?"

"Because you don't get it. You're supposed to want to make the world a better place. Instead you've decided that doesn't matter at all."

"I never promised to be a good person."

"Clearly."

"I don't see what's so wrong with wanting to make a buck."

"I guess you wouldn't," Ash huffed. She was done. Guys like Noah had the world in the palm of their hands. He didn't need to be sensitive to anyone or care about anyone. The world catered to him. If that was power, Ash didn't want it.

That day in coding class, Mr. Basra announced a new part of the final project.

"We've never done anything like this before, but we're adding a new layer. We're going to have you pitch your ideas to the student body. They'll get to vote on which idea is the best one. Your ranking by your peers will be part of your overall score. It's just one more way for us to create transparency and realism. We want to make this fair. But we also want to reflect the way ideas are accepted by the market."

"You totally got this, man." Sam patted Noah's shoulder. Noah's other friends echoed Sam's thought.

Ash looked down. Why did this have to come down to a popularity contest? It made the competition something she couldn't win. She was Garbage Girl, after all. She could already feel the scholarship slipping out of her grasp. She could see herself bussing tables forever. She could see herself never being able to go to university. She'd be stuck in Delta, knowing that

Charming might be right around any corner.

But in some ways, wouldn't that be okay? Ash would have Katrina's tutorials and a community of vigilante coders. She could read books at the library. She wouldn't give up. Her mom wouldn't want her to give up. And Charming would never know that the girl who cleaned her table at a cafe was Ash. She let out a sigh and did her work.

The day seemed to last forever. Ash was aware that she'd been checking her phone a lot. It wasn't to see how many people were logged on, but to see if Charming was. Nothing took her mind off Charming. She had thought about her first thing in the morning when she woke up and throughout the day, replaying every interaction they'd ever had. Talking and messaging with Charming had become so much a part of Ash's life. Now that she knew it wouldn't be happening, there was a void. Emptiness.

After school, Ash didn't want to go home. Or to whatever Ted's house was to her. Whenever she sat in her room all she could do was think about Charming. She headed to the library instead. There was always homework to do. Mounds and mounds of it. She had to get further with her plans for her augmented reality idea. She needed to write a product pitch, a market analysis, and a blueprint for how to begin. The problem was that her laptop couldn't support the project. She kept getting the beach ball of doom every time she tried to do a test run. The SendLove app took up way too much space on her laptop. But Ash didn't trust the school computers. And she wouldn't be able to work into the night if she limited herself to school hours.

As Ash walked to the library, she imagined what it would be like to wear the lenses she wanted to invent. What if, right here, right now, she and her mom could do one of their goofy dances together? What if she could relive that time they rocked out to ABBA on New Year's Eve? They had raided their closets for scarves and sequined tops and high-heeled boots. Her mom even had blue eyeshadow. All night they rehearsed for no one but themselves.

With ABBA's "Waterloo" running through her head, Ash thought about how triumph could rise out of defeat. Just like the phoenix rises from the ashes of its death. She settled in a cubicle at the back of the library. She worked on her plans until the librarian came to tell her it was closing time. It was seven o'clock and dark outside. It was raining and Ash still did not want to go home. She was afraid of running into Noah and Mimi and having to admit defeat. Deep down, she feared she would lie in bed and think about Charming. She was afraid Charming would haunt her dreams. So Ash headed for the Tim Hortons on Scott Road. It was bright and safe. She could keep working there until Noah and Mimi were asleep. Then she could slink into the house like a mouse. That would be her new strategy. Stay out late and only go there to crash for a few hours.

By eleven o'clock her forearms hurt from typing. Her stomach hurt from the coffee, and her butt hurt from sitting still for too long. Ash thought about her options. She needed to make things work at Ted's. There were no other workable options. She would not admit to the government that she had no one. It would make clawing herself out even harder. She scribbled "Make it work" in her notebook.

Ash was ready to pack it in for the night. Her laptop keyboard was hot and she knew she needed to give it a rest. By the time she walked home, it'd be midnight and everyone would be in their rooms. She thought about Charming. Working had made her sure of her choices again. Love would have to wait. She had bigger problems to solve, like how to get through the year. She hoped Charming understood that they could never reveal who they really were. There was no point. Ash walked home in the rain. She told herself over and over that she could make it work.

15 The Enemy of My Enemy

ASH WAS WORKING IN the cafeteria when Mimi's friend Alison came in. She ordered fries. Ash scooped them into the little brown cardboard box.

"Would you like gravy on that?" Ash asked.

"Sure," Alison said. She dug in her purse for her debit card. Then she looked up and said, "Ash — it's Ash, right? Can I ask you something kind of strange?"

Ash nodded.

"What's your final coding project about?"

Ash seized up. Why was Alison curious about that? Was she going to sabotage Ash? Steal the idea? Tell Noah? "Uh . . . why?"

"Because I don't want Noah to win."

"Oh yeah?"

Alison nodded. "Don't think I'm petty or mean. I'm really not. I just . . . Not that guy. It can't be him. And I've been hearing that it'll come down to the two of you."

"You have? It will?" Ash was shocked that people were talking about her. About anything other than her being Garbage Girl. But she couldn't give Alison any false hope. "I think Noah already has it in the bag. I can't compete with him if it comes down to peer rankings. He's too popular."

"Don't be so sure. What's your concept?" She started eating her fries right there, standing at the counter.

Ash eyed the lineup forming behind Alison. "If you really want to know about it, meet me in the library after school."

Ash was in the library doing her homework when Alison joined her.

"You better be kicking butt on that project," she said. "What's it all about?"

Ash let out the tiniest of laughs. She thought it was cool that Alison was invested in her project. But she knew it wasn't about her. It was about Noah. She thought about an episode of *The Office* where Dwight Schrute said, "The enemy of my enemy is my friend." If that was what was at work here, Ash would take it.

"Um . . . I guess you could say it's about talking to dead people." Ash laughed at herself. She had never talked about it with anyone but Charming. Here, in real life, her idea sounded absurd. "It's just my messed up way of trying to keep my mom alive. She died, you know." Of course anyone in Mimi's group would know. *Poor little orphan girl.*

But Ash could see real sympathy in Alison's face. "I'm sorry to hear that."

"Thanks." Ash couldn't go there in her mind. It would make her cry. So she stifled her tears by talking about the work. "Yeah, you know how they're developing glasses that can make you see holograms and stuff like that? I've been thinking, why not use footage of loved ones? You would be able to interact with them. Like instead of watching videos of them over and over, you would see them sitting at the kitchen table again. You could dance with them. That sort of thing."

"That's pretty cool," Alison said.

"Is it?" Ash asked. "I'm not sure it is. Sometimes I think it's kind of creepy. Or that it's, you know, wishful thinking. Something only I would care about. But I just, well, I have to go with my best idea." It wasn't just Ash's best idea. It was her only idea. This late in the year, she had no time to start over. So her doubts didn't change the fact that she had to put everything behind this project.

"You deserve the scholarship way more than Noah does," said Alison.

"So what's your beef with Noah?" Ash asked. "Why do you want to see him fail?"

"He's a horrible human being. He made my life miserable in grade nine."

"He did? How?" Ash could not imagine Alison's life being miserable. She had everything that everyone in high school wanted. Looks. Friends. Money. Good family. Nice clothes. Clear skin. Great natural hair.

"Back when I was all zitty and awkward, I really liked him. I went to a party and we played this stupid kissing game. He refused to kiss me. I wouldn't have minded if he was nice about it. But he humiliated me in front of everyone."

"I had no idea."

"Most people don't know. I was at a different school then. By the time I transferred here, I'd outgrown the person I was then. To be honest, I'm not even sure that Noah knows it was me."

"Wow. Intense."

"Yeah." Alison looked off into a distance beyond the library. "I guess that's why I believe in the whole makeover thing. I changed my look and attitude. And then I came here and my life was suddenly easier. I mean, it's all pretty shallow. But appearances matter."

"I guess." Ash wasn't sure she bought in to that.

"So I was thinking." Alison pulled out her makeup bag. "I'm more than happy to offer some help. We could go to Sephora and get you the extra edge that you might need to win."

"I don't think makeup will make any difference."

"You'd be surprised. I could work on that hair of yours. My sister has clothes that would fit you perfectly."

"Sounds fun," said Ash. "But I'm okay. I don't like makeup. I have no time for hair. Really."

"That's too bad. I was given a five hundred dollar gift certificate to use at Guildford Mall. I want to put it to good use in stopping Noah from winning."

Ash thought about it for a second. "You know what could use a makeover?"

Alison shook her head.

"This guy." Ash patted her laptop. "He's old. This

power cord is about to give out. What I wouldn't give for more memory and a software update."

"Cool. Let's go on the weekend."

Before she logged off and headed home, Ash checked SendLove one last time. There was a message from Charming in her inbox. It was a long message, so she closed it without reading. She might as well be at home for it.

16 Claiming What's Hers

THE HOUSE WAS DARK. No one left the lights on for Ash. And she wouldn't have wanted them to. She took off her shoes by the front door and carried them to her room. She hoped they would not drip onto the hardwood floor and leave marks. She didn't want to leave any sign she was there. She wanted to be totally unseen. Even when she brushed her teeth, she was quiet about it. No one listening would have heard anything but the sound of water going down the drain as she swished the mint froth around in her mouth and gently spit it out.

Ash turned off the light to change. She threw on her RV Park t-shirt in the dark. Just the feel of it reminded her of the time she flashed Charming. She turned on her laptop by feel, logged in to SendLove, and opened Charming's message.

Charming: I could be wrong about this, but I feel our connection is deeper than any I've had with anyone else. I don't want to distract you from your work or get in the way of your goals. But I do want to meet you because I think love is pretty rare. And if you haven't guessed already, I have fallen for you pretty hard. Maybe that's a weird thing to say since we don't know each other. Sometimes I think this is all some cruel joke. But then I remember the sound of your voice and I know you are real. I believe that. Please let me get to know you. In real life.

Love. Ash read the message three times. Every time, that one word caught her eye and her heart. She knew that was what she felt for Charming.

An alert that someone wanted to chat came through. The sound was enough to jolt her alert in the silence of the night. It was Charming.

Charming: I guess you're done with me?

Ash nearly cried. It was so far from the truth. The truth was that she couldn't bear to be a burden on Charming's life.

Cinders: How've you been?
Charming: Good, I guess.

There was a signal that Charming was typing more.

Charming: Were you ever going to get in touch with me again?
Cinders: I've been busy.
Charming: This doesn't feel like a real relationship.
Cinders: I guess it isn't.

Love isn't always enough to make a relationship, Ash thought. It made her sad to admit it, since it had been the best thing she had. Ash was crying. Charming would not want to have anything to do with her if she actually knew Ash. After all, she was Garbage Girl.

Charming: I'm calling you.

Ash's FaceTime dinged.

She didn't know if she should answer. But she did.

Ash had always thought of herself as logical. She made decisions with her head, not her heart. Until now. Everything she had been feeling came spilling out as soon as she started talking with Charming.

"I feel alone," said Ash. "Alone and worried about things I can't even talk to you about."

"What's going on?" Charming asked gently.

"I'm starting to think that I'll never get out of here. I feel like my whole future is at stake. I thought making SendLove would help. But here I am, a victim of online bullying."

"I hate the Internet," Charming said. "It's ruining my life, too. But back to you."

"I hate that I care. Because I honestly don't really care what other people think. I just want to get the hell out of here. SendLove people are doing what they can. But it's not enough and that's such a depressing thought. When will it ever be enough?"

"When people stop hating on each other."

"When will that happen?"

"Honestly? Probably never."

"I don't have time for this. I have actual goals."

"So achieve them. Stand up. Claim SendLove. Whoever it is will leave you alone when they realize they're messing with the wrong person."

"You think?"

"Of course. You have to do this."

Ash had never thought about it that way. But when Charming said it, it made so much sense. Charming believed in Ash.

"What about the haters?" Ash asked.

"Helloo-ooh? Your app is all about that. I mean, if

anyone has something to teach haters, it's you. You have something to share with people who are the target of haters. What's the worst that can happen?"

Ash felt the weight of Charming's words. She couldn't escape her fate. But she could change it. She hated the spotlight. She had avoided it her whole life. But she needed to claim her space. She needed to stand up and be seen as someone other than Garbage Girl.

"Being targeted doesn't scare you?" Ash asked.

"I can think of worse things."

"Are you for real? What could possibly be worse?"

"Oh, all kinds of things. Like being told to stay in the closet. Or being told that the world loves lesbians and to hurry up and be out. Fighting with your parents. Having no idea how to have a career. I'm sorry. That's my shit storm. Let's talk about you more."

"No, what's going on with you?"

"Uh, well . . . I don't know how much of it I can tell you. At least right here, right now."

That was just it, wasn't it? If not right here, right

now, how could they ever find out if what they felt was real?

"This is why I feel like this is going nowhere," said Ash sadly. "We can't talk about anything anymore. If we ever could."

"That's not what I'm saying, Cinders. What I'm asking is if we can meet in person."

"Really?" Ash fought down the panic to what she felt underneath. She wished she could meet Charming. "I didn't think that would ever happen."

"I was getting afraid that it would never happen."

"What's changed?"

"Everything. All the stuff I used to be afraid of doesn't scare me anymore. Instead what scares me is the thought of letting you go. Of letting this pass us by."

"What is this?"

"I think we should find out."

Charming was so brave, Ash had to respond with courage of her own. If Charming dumped her the minute she realized Ash was Garbage Girl, so be it. It was useless to think about it. Ash had to get dressed. And figure out how to get to Brown's Social House. The next bus came by in half an hour. She had to be on it so she could go meet Charming.

17 Face to Face

WHEN THE BUS PULLED to a stop across from the strip mall at 64th and Scott, the brakes let out a loud screech. Ash braced herself. She tucked her chin into her scarf. The back door opened.

There, standing on the sidewalk, was the body Ash had seen on her computer screen. And she looked down into the face of Char Gill. Ash thought about the song Char had sung at the showcase, and Ash's fumbling attempts to tell her how it made her feel. She didn't want to be *that* girl. She wasn't *that* girl. She blushed. Charming was Char. This was both much better and much worse than Ash had thought it would be.

But she had to say something. "Charming?"

"Cinders?"

"You're Char Gill," said Ash. "I was at your showcase performance."

"Oh, yeah. You were working. You said some really nice things about my song."

Ash laughed. "Yep. That's me. My name's Ashley, by the way. Call me Ash."

When Ash extended her hand, Char reached out and took it to shake. "I can't believe you were there while I played a song about you," Char said.

"That song was about me?" Ash had felt the words speaking to her heart. She had known in her soul that the words were for her. But at the time she couldn't make sense of it with her mind. Now it all clicked.

"There's only so many people at our school. I knew you couldn't hide from me forever," Char said.

"That's what I was afraid of," Ash said. "You'd see me and know you were up late chatting and FaceTiming with Garbage Girl."

"That's so not what you are to me. Or to anyone. Cinders, I mean, Ash. Let's go inside. It's too cold to deal with this out here."

Ash followed Char into Brown's. It was one of the places she heard people at school talking about. But Ash had never dreamed of going there. She could never afford to go there. She kept her head down and said nothing. Charming paid the lineup at the entrance no mind as the hostess led them to a table.

"What are you thinking about?" Char asked after they had been seated.

"I just can't believe the song was about me," said Ash. "I'm replaying that moment in my mind. And, well, it was so beautiful."

"I'm so happy you were there to see it."

Ash didn't know what to say. She had zero skills at small talk.

Clearly, Char knew how to handle the small talk

thing. "So your handle," Char said. "Charming isn't much of a stretch. But why Cinders?"

"Cinders. Ash. Makes sense, right? My mom was into mythology. She named me after the phoenix rising from the ashes."

Ash felt bad that she couldn't keep up her side of the conversation. She couldn't put the whole thing on Char. Maybe she should find a reason to leave.

"I shouldn't be here," Ash said.

"Why not?"

"I don't belong at a place like this." Ash gestured at the leather booth, the heavy tablecloths, and the sparkling glassware.

"What? Here?"

"Yeah."

"I don't see the problem."

"You really don't? You're not looking, then. You feel at home in a place like this. I can't. You're way more everything than me. Popular, pretty, confident."

"Don't do this to yourself, Ash. You are hands down the smartest person I know. And the craziest part of all is that you're so humble about it."

Ash felt tears gather in her eyes. "It's hard to hear that you believe in me. We're just very different. Aren't you friends with Mimi?"

"God, no. Can't stand her."

"I thought you were friends. She's always talking about you."

"To you?"

"Not *to* me so much as near me. I live with her and Noah. I'm their stepsister."

It was crazy how Char made Ash feel. Ash had always thought she had girls like Char figured out. They were good at making girls like Ash feel insecure. When Alison was nice to her, Ash didn't know how to handle it. But she was even more out of her depth here. To think that she and Char Gill had done what they'd done online and talked about what they'd talked about. It was all so much to take in.

And she thought Char must feel the same way. Now that they were face to face, it seemed clear that they couldn't be together. Ash and Char lived in different worlds. The only place those worlds met was at school, and that way lay disaster. Everything about her felt exposed.

Ash saw Char look at her, then down at the ground. Of course, Char felt awkward about this, too. Ash didn't know what to say to make it better. She told herself that it wouldn't take long to clear up this cosmic mistake. She could be on her way home again within the hour. The server asked what they wanted. Char ordered for both of them.

"I'm glad you're here," Char said.

"You are?" Ash asked.

Ash swallowed hard. Everything she was weighed her down, held her in place. She felt the weight of her second-hand sweater, the jeans she got out of a free bin. She could even feel the touch of lipstick she was wearing. It was a tube that someone had left on their tray in the cafeteria. There was still some left in the tube. So Ash kept it instead of taking it to the lost and found. Even the memories of that moment said way too much about her. She wished she'd just tossed the thing and didn't have it dabbed on her lips. She pressed her lips together as if to remind herself that she was out of place.

"I've never met anyone like you."

Ash thought that Char meant she'd never met anyone so pathetic, but she kept that to herself.

"You are who you are," Char went on. "And that's so cool. And you're so not trying to be cool."

"You're right about that," Ash said. "I accepted not being cool a long time ago."

"Which is what makes you so cool."

"You think?" What was Char talking about? Not cool was not cool.

"I can't believe you. Look at SendLove. You created a cure for online bullying. Do you have any idea how amazing that is? And you don't want to make money or fame off it. You're a really good person. I didn't know there was such a thing."

"You didn't?"

"Hell no. Everything around me is toxic. My family is a mess. Even my so-called friends. Other than my friend Everett. He's cool. But I'm so done with this scene. I just want to do my own thing now."

"You will. You have to. You have such a beautiful voice all on your own. I was blown away that night I first heard you."

"When I sang about you." Char smiled.

18 Different Worlds

THEY LEFT THE RESTAURANT together. The air was cool, but the thick layer of fog made the night feel warm.

They walked down 64th and turned on Wade Road. They talked about everything and anything. Ash forgot that she had been awed by Char. Instead she rode the wave of excitement she felt at being with her. Char held Ash in her arms, and Ash felt warmer and safer than she had since her mom died. They shared a quick kiss, and Ash wanted more.

A part of Ash didn't know what she was doing. None of it made sense. Char was so far out of her reality, Ash couldn't get her head around it. How could there be a world in which they were even in the same room, let alone pressing their lips together? Ash took it all in. The absurdity of their meeting. The butterflies she'd felt from words and voices exchanged online. It was all so far-fetched, but it was real. Ash had no idea how much time had passed. Time had no meaning. Where they were had no meaning, until Char said, "Let's get out of here."

When they went to pass the bus stop, Char grabbed Ash by the arm. They stopped in the middle of the sidewalk and stared at each other.

Char looped her fingers into Ash's jeans and pulled their hips close to each other. Ash had never stood so close to anyone. She felt a rush that she could not describe. It was pure longing. Char looked into her eyes. "Come here."

This time the kiss was deeper, more passionate. Ash could feel the warmth spread from her lips through her whole body. Their tongues met and melted together. When they finally pulled apart, Ash felt like she was losing a piece of herself.

They held hands as Char led Ash to the parking lot. Char's car was the cutest orange Fiat Ash had ever seen. Ash thought that everything about Char was like something in a romance story or a fairy tale. Char opened the door to let Ash in. She put her hand up to Ash's cheek and they melted together into a kiss again. And then Char took Ash home to her place.

Char's room was off in its own private area of the house. Ash felt like she knew this place as well as she knew Char. But really being there made her feel like she had been plunked down on an alien world. How could she go from here back to her storage closet of a room at Ted's?

"I can't do this," Ash said.

She tried to explain to Char. It wasn't that Char was anything but perfect. It wasn't that they were both girls. It was that neither of them could escape her own life. Neither of them could escape who she was. Char was like a princess. Her whole realm lay before her, waiting for her to claim. Ash was the Garbage Girl. She lived her life peddling trash. Even the coding she loved was part of that world. SendLove was made to clear out the garbage online. Her augmented reality project was about making the waste of her life more livable.

"It's not you," Ash said to Char. "Trust me when I tell you it's not you. I have to go."

She grabbed her coat and was out the door.

Ash was awake but still in bed. She wanted to pull the covers over her head and let the world go on without her. If life was a roller coaster, it was time for her to get off and barf.

Noah opened her door.

"No. Not today. Go away," Ash ordered. She turned over and refused to look at him.

"We have to talk about the project."

"No, we don't. I'm not doing it."

"You don't have that option." His voice was threatening.

It was the same scam he'd pulled before. But Ash was smarter now. And she had hit bottom. The lower she sank and the less she had to lose, the easier it was to defy him.

"I'm not doing your work, Noah. And there's nothing you can do about it. Run to your daddy if you want. But I'm not lifting a finger for you anymore."

There. She was done.

"But . . . but . . ."

She pulled the covers up until she was invisible. It was her final message to him. It was the ultimate *go away*. And he did.

She thought about what would happen if he did tell Ted. What did any of it matter anymore? Ash was heartbroken. That was worse than any of this.

But Ash had to get up. She was meeting Alison.

Getting a new laptop was out of the question. But the old charger cord just could not hold any longer. The duct tape on the cord was getting to be a safety hazard. Ash was afraid of starting a fire.

She and Alison went to the Apple Store and pulled out her old clunker.

The clerk, a guy about her age, laughed at her. "I'm amazed this thing still works. It's antique."

"My mom bought it for me when I turned twelve."

"She hasn't heard of upgrading?"

"My mom died. I can't afford to upgrade. I just need a new cord." Ash surprised herself with her bluntness. But she never could handle anyone trying to play her.

The guy's face changed completely. "I'm sorry," he said. He looked like he meant it. "Listen, we don't sell these anymore. But I'll see what I can do. Wait here."

Ash browsed the sleek new models. She ran her fingers across the brand new MacBook Pro. This was her dream. One day, she'd have the equipment to be able to do everything she needed to do.

Just then the guy returned with the cord. "So you're really still running this old operating system?"

"Yeah."

Alison broke in. "And the crazy part is, she's some kind of computer nerd. Hey, is there anything you can do to make it better with a five hundred dollar gift card?"

"Of course," said the computer guy.

"Let's do it," Alison said.

It was all too much. Ash would be able to do everything she needed to do. She'd be able to create the vision for her final product.

As she and Alison walked out of the Apple store, Ash beamed. She couldn't wait to get home to work. But she wanted to hang out with Alison a little longer, too. They went to Purdy's and got ice cream bars dipped in chocolate and almonds.

"So you actually live with Noah and Mimi," Alison said.

"Yeah."

"Sounds awful."

"It's temporary. I mean, I'll leave in June."

"Ash, I don't believe you. I just gave you the perfect set up to bitch them out. And you didn't."

Ash shrugged. "I could. But I decided a while back that I wouldn't let them drag me down."

"Good for you. I get that. I'm kind of sick of Mimi and the rest of the girls. It's the negativity."

"It's soul sucking."

"Yeah," Alison said, taking a bite of her ice cream. "You know what? You're okay, Ash."

They stood surrounded by chocolate treats. They ate their ice cream and laughed when the crunchy layer started to fall apart. They knew they had to eat fast or the whole thing would fall apart.

19 Lost and Found

ASH'S NEW FRIENDSHIP WITH Alison saved her from losing all hope in humanity. But she went over the events of that night with Char with a fine-tooth comb and could not get any of it to make sense. The leaving, yes. But how did they even get together? The only explanation she could come up with was that they got swept up in something supernatural. And now that the spell was over, Ash had one option. She had to forget it. She had to go back to her goals and her work. That was all she could count on in life. There was no such thing as romance for people like her.

She ducked into the back of the cafeteria using keys Sally had given her. Three large clear bags of cans had been stashed there. Ash took one bag over her shoulder and held another in front with the same hand. The tops of both bags were clutched in her right hand over her left shoulder. The other bag, she held with her left hand.

She walked through the streets of Delta to the recycling depot. She didn't even care if anyone was filming her. What did that matter? This was her life. There was no point fighting it. All those years with her mom, she had learned that life was about hard work and being a good person. She was grateful for what her mom taught her.

Ash thought about Noah and Mimi. Their mom was off living in Switzerland without them. They were awful to her, but she felt sorry for them. Maybe she would have a mean and cold heart, too, if her mom had left her. Instead, Ash had the kind of focus and drive that her mom would be proud of.

But then she remembered how touched her mom was when Ted was kind to her. It had seemed clear to Ash that her mom would have disapproved of her wasting all that time on Char. But as she walked to the depot, she became less and less sure. Ash could almost hear her mom telling her that she worked so hard. Too hard. Her mom would say that she deserved to have fun now and then. She would tell her that life is about connection, that we sometimes find it in unexpected places with unexpected people.

Ash was riddled with guilt for having walked out on Char. It was a cruel thing to do. But she had no choice but to run. She relived that moment. It was like the façade had crumbled and she was standing there, naked, in front of Char. All Ash's defects, all her weaknesses in full view. That was no way to be seen by the person you most wanted to impress. Bolting had been her only option.

Char's life had to be easier. She might talk about her family and their challenges. But they were people who provided for her and protected her in ways that Ash would never know again. Ash was on her own. It made it hard to relate to other kids at school. But she could hear her mom's voice telling her not to isolate herself, not to feel different or cast out. Char hadn't been casting her out. Why had Ash been so willing to do it to herself?

In her mind's eye, Ash saw her mom and herself walking together. She even imagined her mom offering to carry one of the bags. Ash silently told her that she couldn't, because she was an apparition. But in a way, she was real. Ash could talk to her, be with her, and tell her everything in her heart. It didn't matter if other people couldn't understand that or see her mom there. This was private. This was her own inner world. And if all went well, one day she would create the tools to bring that inner world to life. That in itself was worth living for. But there was a voice in Ash's head — maybe her mom's? — telling her there was more to life than that.

Ash got to the recycling depot and took her money. She stuffed the cash into her pocket and left the place with a sense of lightness. It was a relief not to have to carry those bags.

She was crossing the parking lot when she felt a presence come up beside her. She turned to see an orange Fiat. Char was staring at her from the driver's side. She rolled down her window.

"Hey," Char called out into the cold.

Ash turned. "What are you doing here?"

"I hope I didn't scare you."

"You did a little. What are you doing here?" Ash repeated. She just couldn't believe that Char had appeared out of nowhere like that.

Char shrugged. "I don't know. Giving you a lift home?"

Ash wasn't sure what was happening. But she decided she was too tired to fight it. She got in the car and they drove off. Sitting there, surrounded by warmth, she listened to Char talk. She let Char make her laugh. She realized that she had a chance to make up for the night before.

"Char, I'm sorry for what I did last night," said

Ash, looking down at her lap. "It was kind of messed up to lead you on like that and then run away."

"You did what you had to do. Do you feel different today?"

Nothing had changed really. But in that moment, Ash knew everything she needed to know. They were right for each other. They would figure out whatever they needed to figure out.

After stopping at Char's house to pick up her guitar, they headed for the beach. There, beneath the shelter of a tree, Char played a song for Ash. It was about the nights they spent with each other. It was about falling in love with the idea of a girl and being afraid of being real. It was about the girl leaving and having to live with heartbreak. It was about still loving the girl. It was so honest that Ash cried when she heard it. It made her cry harder when she saw that Char had broken down, too.

Ash was filled with pride for Char being brave enough to share it. She didn't even try to hide how much the song and Char singing just for her meant to her.

Back in the car Ash insisted on hearing the song one more time. This time she used her phone to record it.

"I'm sorry I freaked out last night," Ash said.

"So you like me again?" Char asked.

"Of course I like you. I never stopped liking you. I just thought you were too good for me."

"Why would you say something like that?" Char pulled Ash closer to her. Over the gearshift, they got really close, kissable close. Then Char whispered, "You're everything I've ever dreamed of."

"Am I really?" Ash asked. "How come I don't believe you?"

"Because you're humble. Because you have no idea how amazing you are."

They kissed.

Ash had to talk Char into posting the video online. The song was perfect. Char was perfect. And Ash wanted the world to see her.

They kissed again.

Later that afternoon, they pulled up in front of Char's house. Ash didn't know how to behave. She didn't know what to do with herself. Meeting Char's family was a big deal. And she was dressed for the recycling depot in her ratty old thrift store clothes.

But they made it easy on her. Everyone was really kind, especially Char's dad. He wanted to know all about Ash's projects. He asked her about her future.

20 Winning

IT WAS THE MORNING OF graduation. Ash took a deep breath. She looked at herself in the mirror. She was different now. She knew more about the world and the people in it. She knew there were people who would take advantage of power, who made other people's lives miserable just because they could. But there were also people like Alison and all the members of SendLove. There were people like Char.

"Morning, babe," Char said as Ash climbed into